Loyalty Ain't Promised 2

Keith Williams

Lock Down Publications and Ca$h
Presents
Loyalty Ain't Promised 2
A Novel by *Keith Williams*

Keith Williams

Lock Down Publications
P.O. Box 944
Stockbridge, Ga 30281

Copyright 2020 Keith Williams
Loyalty Ain't Promised 2

Lock Down Publications
Like our page on Facebook: Lock Down Publications @
www.facebook.com/lockdownpublications.ldp
Cover design and layout by: **Dynasty Cover Me**
Book interior design by: **Shawn Walker**
Edited by: **Kiera Northington**

Stay Connected with Us!

Text **LOCKDOWN** to 22828 to stay up-to-date with new releases, sneak peaks, contests and more...

Thank you!

Submission Guideline.

Submit the first three chapters of your completed manuscript to ldpsubmissions@gmail.com, subject line: Your book's title. The manuscript must be in a .doc file and sent as an attachment. Document should be in Times New Roman, double spaced and in size 12 font. Also, provide your synopsis and full contact information. If sending multiple submissions, they must each be in a separate email.

Have a story but no way to send it electronically? You can still submit to LDP/Ca$h Presents. Send in the first three chapters, written or typed, of your completed manuscript to:

LDP: Submissions Dept
P.O. Box 944
Stockbridge, Ga 30281

DO NOT send original manuscript. Must be a duplicate.

Provide your synopsis and a cover letter containing your full contact information.

Thanks for considering LDP and Ca$h Presents.

Dedication:

This book is dedicated to everybody in this crazy world who feel as if loyalty doesn't exist anymore. I'm here to tell you that it does. You just can't be the one to expect it from everybody, because most of the time we have bad judgement of people and expect too much from the wrong people, even if they are family.

Keith Williams

Chapter 1

E'Mani

"Newman! Newman!" *Boom*! *Boom*! *Boom*! *Boom*! "Wake your ass up, it's count time," Officer Davis kicked my cell door and yelled in her annoying ass voice. I got up but cursed under my breath, hating the fact she woke me up after I had just made it to sleep. I took two deep breaths, then got up to wash my face after she passed my room. I was so fuckin stressed it didn't even make sense. It's been two long months since the day I was booked into this nasty ass jail in Pinellas County, and the day I fought Ashlyn.

If you all haven't read part one, let me be the first to tell you, these pussy ass cops are holding me against my own free will because Ashlyn and Alice, two bitches I thought were my friends dropped a dime on me. They said I was an accessory to Supreme's murder.

I walked to the door to look out the window into the hallway after washing my face. I really don't know why, they had just called count so there wasn't anybody out there, but it was a habit I picked up the short time I've been here. Once I was back on my bunk, I stared at the ceiling thinking about my life and where it was headed. Besides first appearance, I still haven't been to court and it was literally driving me insane, not knowing anything about my own fuckin case.

I could still hear the judge's voice ringing in my head as he clearly stated my chance for a bail was being denied. He knew, whatever he set, I would've been out this bitch by the time the ink dried on his paperwork.

Then, my mother is still upset with me for getting myself in this situation and she almost disclaimed me, until she saw the support the church was giving us. I felt she was being real selfish, because all she thought about was me embarrassing her, not about saving her daughter's life. The hatred I felt for her was something I had never felt before and it was kind of scaring me. I recently stopped accepting her visits to keep my stress level down and as hard as it was for me to deny my mother, it was something I had to do.

Once count cleared, I was told I had an attorney visit. Surprised, but happy as hell. I knew my girl Mahogany came through for me. Double B's for life, bitch! I was cuffed and led to the room to talk with my lawyer. A short but muscular white man introduced himself as Michael Conn and then told me something I had already figured he was paid by Mahogany to defend me.

From his appearance, I knew he would be about business when he stepped in front of the judge, because he was Jewish. And like all real Jews, he wore one of them miniature hats on top of his head, I think they call it a yarmulke.

We went over everything, ending with him explaining that the D.A. had a weak case. All they had was hearsay, but if we took it to trial, it was still possible the jury could believe the witnesses. I thought about what he said and again, I couldn't believe these bitches dropped a dime on me. They had to disappear. My damn life was on the line.

Once my visit was over, I walked back to my cell with my head held high as lesbians made cat calls at me. I really wasn't in the mood for their bullshit, so I kept walking not saying a word. until one of them bitches screamed my name. The two officers grabbed both of my arms and damn near dragged me before I had a chance to turn around, but the minute I rounded the corner, Ashlyn stared me in the eyes. I couldn't believe it, for a minute I thought my eyes were playing tricks on me, but as I looked back one last time, I could see it was definitely Ashlyn.

There were so many emotions I was feeling at once, I swear I going to lose my mind like young Jeezy. Again, not only was I in here because of her, but she was the reason I was on protected custody. She illustrated on my ass so bad when I blacked out, the officers thought I got jumped so I was put on P.C.

Back in my cell, I paced like I was a caged animal, looking for my first opportunity to escape. I wanted out of this place while I was sane enough to still have control of my own mind. I've heard too many stories where people go crazy in places like this and most of them ended with the person never being the same once they're released. I was too fly for this shit, and for the life of me, I still couldn't understand how I let myself end up in a situation like this. I didn't deserve this shit. Yeah, I fucked up and may have fucked over a couple people, but I still didn't deserve this, and that's how I fuckin felt. I smiled to myself because I was really about to lose it in this cell, I needed to get myself together real quick because this was not a game I was really locked up in a fuckin jail cell, facing life in prison.

That meant there's a chance I may never see the light of day again. I sat down on my bunk, because just the thought of spending the rest of my life locked up made me nauseous. *Damn, what the hell did I get myself into?* I thought again as tears started to blur my vision. I can't do life in prison, that's out the question. I can't snitch either, that's definitely out the question, so I have to come up with a way to get rid of Ashlyn and Alice.

"Newman, get yourself together, you have a visit in five minutes," Officer Davis said over the speaker. I got up off my bunk and rushed to the door. I needed to inform her that I was refusing my visit, because I knew it could only be one person and that was my mother.

"Officer Davis! Officer Davis! May I talk to you for a minute?" She sucked her teeth and after taking her precious time, she finally made it to my door almost ten minutes later.

"What, Newman?" she snapped.

"Can you let the transport officer know I'm refusing my visit?" I know it might sound crazy me not wanting to see my mother, but please don't judge me because nobody knows like I do and besides, I do what the fuck I want."

"Oh hell no, Newman, I'm about to go home, that means my shift is over and the remaining twenty minutes I'm not doing any paperwork, so there is no refusing visits, no pissing me off and no getting on my damn nerves, you understand? So, get ready for your visit. I don't know why anybody would come visit your stupid ass anyway," she said, before walking off. That bitch always had something smart to say, I guess because I was locked up, she thought she was better than me. When I get out, she just better not let me catch her by herself.

I freshened up and got ready for my visit, then mentally got ready for my mother. It wasn't five minutes before one of the same officers who took me to see my lawyer, showed up to escort me to my visit. He made me walk in front of him this time, just so he could stare at my ass, and being that I knew he was looking, I threw an extra sway in my hips while making my ass stick out a little more than normal. All men are dogs and dogs will fuck anything with a hole, so it didn't surprise me when I peeped over my shoulders and saw his eyes glued to my ass while he grabbed his dick.

I smiled, because I just proved to myself that even though I was in a jail uniform, I still could make a man fantasize about E'mani Newman. To all my sistas in the free world, always remember the outfit don't make a bad bitch, a bad bitch makes the outfit.

I was so caught up in myself, the moment I turned the corner into the visiting area, I broke down in tears. My girl Mahogany stood there like she was posing for the cover of *Black Men Magazine*, with a big smile on her face.

"Girl, what you crying for? I know you ain't happy to see me," she asked as I picked up the receiver and put it to my ear.

I tried to reply but got choked up, so I took a deep breath to calm myself down then tried again. "Mahogany, girl, I swear you just made my day. You have no idea how much I miss you, and to think, I was about to refuse my visit." She let me vent for a while, until I spilled all my emotions on her and cried until I had no more tears to cry. I really needed that, because there was so much built up inside of me, a nervous breakdown was soon to come and that I didn't need.

"Well, since you're done, I thought I might need give you the run down about what's been going on. First, I gotta inform you that we added two more bitches to the roster," she said, referring to recruiting two more Baller Babies. "Their names are Champagne and Passion, and these bitches are no joke. Passion kind of reminds me of you though, she's a mixed breed white and black so every once in a while, I catch her talking all proper and shit like you used to do.

I had been hearing about them for a while from my brother, but get this, I heard they had the city of Gainesville on lock.

"You know I had Sweatt do a PSI to make sure these bitches were solid though, and come to find out, they ain't the one to be fucked up with if you're not on the same team as them. The other thing is that CoCo said she had to go home for a little while, so she haven't been around. She should be back in a couple months though. I know one thing; she better have her ass back when it's time to go handle business. You know it's Double B's before anything."

I laughed because Mahogany was a straight up alpha female when it came to the Baller Babies.

"Alright now, bitch, you over there laughing and shit and you got these snitching ass hoes about to take the stand on your ass. I got a plan though, but first I gotta ask, do you trust me?" she said, while staring me in the eyes through the thick plexiglass that separated us.

I met her stare and thought hard about her question. I mean, Mahogany had always looked out for me and even when Neeko kidnapped me, it was Mahogany who found him to help me get my revenge. Then again, the bitch was fucking my man. Yeah, Supreme was my man, I didn't give a damn if he was with her for eight years or not. To sum it all up though, the good outweighed the bad. So yes, I can say I trusted her with my life.

"Yes, I trust you. I trust you to do what you always do. I trust you to be you," I stated, still not turning away from our stare down. We continued this for a couple seconds longer, I guess, so she could read me to see if I lying or not, but my answer was genuine.

"Well, the next time Michael Conn come to visit you, tell him you want to push for a speedy trial," Mahogany told me. I stood there thinking about what she just said and like an on switch, my tears started falling again.

"Why would I do that? This is my life we talking about, Mahogany. I can't—"

Before I could finish my sentence, she cut me off like what I was saying didn't matter. "I got you. E'mani, you said you trust me to be me? Well, let me do me. I just can't get into all the details right now, but you coming home, long as you do what I told you to do."

To keep myself from crying any longer, I winked at her and stated, "I am my bitches' keeper," before bursting into laughter. She started laughing with me and at that moment I felt stress free. I felt like nothing mattered to me, but the bond Mahogany and I shared, because it was definitely a bond that could never be broken.

"Maybe when you get out of here, you can finally get your Double B tattoo," Mahogany said to break the ice. I smiled, because after everything I've been through on behalf of the Baller Babies, I really do think I deserve it.

"You damn right, I'm getting my tattoo. I been thinking about how I'm gone get it and all," I replied. Soon as the words left my mouth, the male officer returned.

"Newman, time's up, tell your family bye and let's get going." I said my goodbyes and walked off with my head down once I hung up the receiver. Before I could get too far from her vision, I heard a loud bang on the plexiglass window. The officer and I both turned around, wondering what the hell was going on and the moment Mahogany's eyes met mine, all I heard was, "Double B's bitch!" And I could do nothing but smile as I walked away.

Chapter 2

Mahogany

"What's up my bitches?" I shouted as I stood in front of Nah Nah, Nicole and Shanel's gravesites. It had been a whole two months since the day they were put to rest and since that dreadful day, I can't lie, I been missing the hell out of them. Once I left the county jail from visiting E'mani, I drove straight here only stopping to pick up some fresh red and white roses.

"I know y'all bitches surprised to see me, but let's keep this shit real, did y'all really think I would forget about y'all? I mean, after everything we've been through, from being locked up in the Florida Institution for Teenage Girls, to taking over Deland and St. Petersburg, Florida. We rocked out like real bitches supposed to. I just hate y'all lives got taken in the process." I finally laid a red and white rose on each of their gravesites before kissing their tombstones.

"It's a lot of shit been going on since y'all been gone and right now, I don't even know where to start from. Well, I'll start with the good stuff. The night after the funeral, E'mani, CoCo and I all went out to Club Paid and showed our asses. I mean, we really balled like the Baller Babies are known for doing. I know y'all remember our homeboy, DJ Red Eyes. Well, he had the club turned out, introducing us over the mic when we walked in and all making us look like celebrities. We even had our own table filled with liquor, I'm talking every kind you can think of, so y'all know we were ballin out of control. We made sure to pour some out for y'all bitches though, it was only right, y'all are still my favorite bitches."

I laughed at myself because I knew my girls were laughing at me and then out of nowhere, I started crying, thinking about them and how our lives turned out. "Man, y'all bitches making me cry and you knew I don't do this crying shit," I laughed again, then continued.

"Now for the bad news. I know, I know, who the fuck like bad news? But hey, I gotta tell y'all hoes everything. So, after we left the club, which was about six in the morning, everything just went downhill. We got to the house still feeling tipsy, well I was kind of horny too, but that's another story. The minute we were on our way up the stairs, we heard somebody banging on the front door like the damn police, so you know we were pissed the fuck off.

"We started to just let them keep knocking, but E'mani nosy ass went to answer it. Man, what I'm about to say next is going to blow y'all damn minds, hold up we may need a moment of silence for this." I stopped talking then bowed my head for about ten seconds, before starting again.

"Okay, here it go. When E'mani opened the door, guess who it was? Yeah, you bitches guessed right, it was the damn police and they locked E'mani ass up for accessory to the murder of Supreme." I just knew my girls were turning over in their graves when I told them that. Yeah, the goody two shoes, church girl E'mani. That's something you couldn't believe unless you saw it but coming out of my mouth, you know that shit couldn't be nothing but the truth.

"Y'all hoes can calm down now, I just left from visiting her and she's alright. She got a little baller baby in her, so the bitch ain't green like she was when we first met. She did get her ass beat though. Yeah, the first day she got there a bitch got on her ass, so right now she's on protected custody. I know that gives the Baller Babies a bad name but trust me, what I have planned, they can kiss the baby because the world will remember us until they are dead and gone, and even then their kids gone talk about us." I sat there quiet for a little while longer, thinking about how I was going to explain something that nobody who's a part of a group wants to hear. It really wasn't no easy way to put it, so I'll just have to come out and say it.

"Y'all hoes know I recruited two more girls. Before I continue, let me say this though. They are not taking y'all place, they could never do that. I just needed some help, but these bitches are the real deal. Yeah, they're bad bitches, so y'all ain't got to question that, and their names are Champagne and Passion." I laughed out loud at myself, because I didn't know if they were thinking the same thing, but it just hit me that Champagne and Passion both sounded like stripper's names. I made a mental note to ask them about that. I mean, it's not a problem, but you know strippers be on that girl-on-girl shit, and trust me when I say we don't need another Kayla in the group.

"Oh yeah, Shanel, you know your twin been missing you like crazy. I really do think a part of her left when you left. She's been depressed a lot lately, so she went back to Panama City with your mother for a little while, she say she wanted to be with family. That part I really didn't get because after all we been through, I could've sworn we were family. I mean, blood couldn't make us no closer to being family then we already were. But I let her go and gave her space to clear her mind. I just hope she realize it's still love over here and we all we got, ain't nothing change."

I went over a couple more things before telling them about my lack of sex life. I knew they were laughing at my ass, because Mahogany not having no dick was kind of like believing a cow really jumped over the moon, but the shit was true. My mind had been all over the place lately and the one time I did get some, I didn't even get a chance to get off. His one-minute ass was worse than Supreme. At least Supreme was a golden head.

I said my last words, then kissed their tombstones again before parting ways. I had to get myself on point though, because I swear I wanted to cry in the car and let everything out like E'mani did when I went to visit her. I never knew life could be so hard. Yeah, I had more than the average woman but after losing three sisters in the same year, it's like my life is left with a big hole in it.

Once I left from seeing my girls, I drove to Mr. Conn's office to go over a couple things regarding E'mani's case. I could tell she really didn't trust me like she said she does, but how I felt didn't really matter. Long as she does what I told her to do, I'll prove to her that she should never question what I say.

"Good afternoon, Mahogany." Mr. Conn greeted me with a handshake once I was let into his office. "How may I assist you today?" I wanted to get straight to the point because honestly, I really didn't know how much time I had.

"Mr. Conn, you've been doing business with Supreme and me for what, about five years now, right?" I asked, stopping to look him in his eyes. Once he shook his head to indicate I was right, I continued. "So, you wouldn't mind giving me a hand with two of your clients. Their names are Ashlyn and Alice Wright and they're charged with first-degree murder, but I know you also know they're both snitching on E'mani." He shook his head again, only this time he stopped me before I could continue.

"No need to go on. I understand what needs to be done, just tell me what you need me to do." I looked at him surprised, and at that moment gained a new level of respect for him. I guess Supreme taught him a little something too before he left this world.

"Address to their father's house, the man who's paying you to defend them," I stated and just like that, I was on my way back to my car.

If the world hasn't figured out by now, I'm the new baddest bitch and Trina needed to respect that. Otherwise, just like her, all you hating ass hoes, bitches or whatever you want to be called can eat a dick. I rode through the city, just to kill time and catch a little breeze before I went home and did nothing. Honestly, I really didn't want to be in that big ass house by myself, but what other choice did I have?

"No smoke! No smoke!" NBA YoungBoy shouted as my cell phone rang. I turned into the nearest park before answering because I knew it could only be one person.

"Talk to me," I stated once I tapped the screen, already feeling annoyed.

"What's poppin, sis? I need a favor from you and before you tell me you can't do it, hear me out first." *I can't believe this shit,* I thought as I took the phone away from my ear and looked at it as if it was a foreign object. After weeks of not hearing from this fool, my brother Sweatt calls and the first thing he does is ask for a favor, no how I been or none of that.

"Oh, I'm doing good, bruh, thanks for asking. Nobody's trying to kill me," I said sarcastically so he would get the vibe I was throwing at him. He gave a light chuckle, I guess catching my drift before apologizing.

"My bad, sis, I just got a lot on—"

"No! You was just thinking about yourself as always, with your ungrateful selfish ass," I snapped, stopping him before he could tell me one of his bullshit ass lies. I loved my brother to death and any bitch that knew me knew that, but sometimes a bitch wasn't with the bullshit, no matter who it was coming from.

"Damn, I guess it's that time of the month, huh? Listen, sis, when you're done PMSing or whatever it is y'all women call it, hit my line because I need your assistance, it's important," Sweatt shot back, but before he could hang up I stopped him.

"Any second after the present is not promised, so let me know what's on your mind." I could hear him inhale before exhaling deeply, I guess letting out the frustration he was feeling after dealing with me. One thing about Sweatt though, he knew out of all people, if I could help him in any way I would and if I couldn't, I'll damn sure risk my freedom trying.

"I need some work put in. Well, it's not really for me, it's for Mr. Montoya, but I can't let him know I'm not about to handle it," he said, then stopped. I knew he was trying to see if I had something smart to say, but I didn't, my brother needed help. Once he realized I was for him and not against him, he continued.

"His name is Gio and he's a five foot eleven Cuban, so he won't be that hard to spot. He owns a jewelry store in Gainesville called Cuban Ice, but only women are allowed in the store. No men, which is why I need your help. He's been doing business with Mr. Montoya for a while now but got too big for his pants, and bit the hand that fed him, which were Mr. Montoya's words. Mr. Montoya wants him taken care of and anything you get out the store is yours. Do you think you can handle that?"

I thought about it, which I really didn't have to, because I could take care of that in my panties and bra. I just wanted to make him sweat.

"Say less, baby brother, you can consider it done. I'll have Champagne and Passion take care of that in the next couple days, but best believe you owe me one," I said, meaning every word and believe me, I do plan on collecting in the near future. We went back and forth again for a little while, this time in a joking matter. He just didn't know that at any time, I was ready to go from zero to a hundred on his ass. He laughed once I told him, but we both knew how true that statement was.

After a while, we finally said our goodbyes before hanging up. Then I found myself watching the little kids in the park running around like they had no care in the world, because they didn't. That made me think about one day settling down and have some children of my own. I fumbled with a couple names and then thought about who they would favor more, me or their daddy.

Sounding crazy as hell, I laughed to myself about what I was just thinking, while I retrieved the blunt of Loud in my armrest. Yeah, believe it. Yours truly turned into a real deal pot head and everybody can thank CoCo's ass for that. Once E'mani got arrested, it was just CoCo and me in the house and the way she smoked, I felt like I didn't have any other choice.

I closed all four windows and blasted the A.C. before putting the flame to my blunt. I wanted to have no worries like the kids who played in front of me, so I had no choice but to hot box this bitch, and that's just what I did as I lay my seat all the way back, took a big pull and then inhaled the thick smoke.

"I don't wanna smoke with nobody! I don't wanna chill with nobody! I don't wanna ride with nobody! I just don't feel like being around nobody!" I sang along with the Ice Billion Berg from the group Dunk Ryders as his solo hit song, "Smoke With Nobody" blasted through my speakers, because that's just how the fuck I felt.

Two blunts and an hour later, I was fumbling around for my car keys. Day had quickly turned into night and the park was empty as if no one had ever been there. Once I finally got myself together, I started the car and drove home to sleep the night away alone.

Chapter 3

Champagne

"Champagne and Passion, bitch! Y'all hoes better remember the names, because if we have to come back out there, ain't gone be no talkin, just bullets flying from my muthafuckin nine," I shouted to the four hoes who called themselves trying to jump on Passion's little sister.

Standing a short five feet tall, with a sexy cappuccino skin complexion, I was what you would call a bad ass bitch, no questions asked. My shoulder-length hair complemented my panther-slit eyes and my body made a lot of niggas feel like they were bulletproof as they say they would go to war, just for a chance to have me. I don't blame them, but what I think really made niggas lust over me even more was the fact that I was a Baller Baby, so they thought they could use me as a come-up, stupid muthafuckas.

Passion, on the other hand, was a mixed breed, white and black to be exact. So, she was one of them high-yella bitches, but with her hazel eyes and slightly bowlegged stance, she was a bad bitch who had natural beauty. She stood an inch or two taller than I did, with about the same amount of ass and hips, so you can imagine me and her together was like Hurricane Katrina in the middle of New Orleans.

We were puttin on for our city as always, but as the new members of the Baller Babies, we had to show Mahogany ballin was like a second nature to us. This a message we're sending to the whole fuckin world, if you ain't with us then you're against us, so that means all y'all bitches are fair game.

We jumped back into my Beemer and I pulled off, turning the corner just as the police arrived on the scene. It never fails. I knew somebody would call the police once they saw my gun, but I had papers for my shit, so I was legit. The world just better get their minds right and remember what my favorite rapper Plies said about riding with your fye or staying your ass home, because I am and will always be a street bitch so the street law I live by, on gang.

We dropped Passion's little sister off at home so we could get ready for nightfall. Right before we had to go save Passion's sister, I had just got off the phone with Mahogany and she gave us our first mission as a Baller Baby. I broke everything down to Passion, not leaving out a single detail, because we needed things to go smooth. We weren't new to this, but I had to admit before we met Mahogany, we were sloppy as hell with our shit. Now, we had a little class.

I beeped the horn and waved my hand as Passion's loudmouth ass yelled bye to her sister out the window. I always hated when she did that shit. I don't know why, but it just fucks with me. It wasn't long before we made it to my place to get dressed because we were still in our "beat a bitch ass" outfits and to make it past the door of this mission, we had to be on our grown and sexy.

We both took a quick shower, with me throwing on a black strapless dress afterwards. My dirty .25 handgun was strapped to my thigh, and the way my silver pumps complimented my toned legs made me want to fuck myself.

Passion, on the other hand, explained that a dress would only slow her down. She felt more comfortable in a pair of tight black jeans, a fitted tee that showed just enough cleavage and a pair of black, thigh-high boots where she kept her Russian twenty-two. I explained to her one more time how important this was, as she lashed out on me for talkin too damn much before walking off. I laughed because I was thinking the same thing, but I was just so obsessed with impressing Mahogany that I needed no room for mistakes. She drove while I rode shotgun and for the hundredth time, checked my clip, making sure I was on full.

Once arriving to Cuban Ice jewelry store, we both applied a coat of cherry red "fuck-me" lipstick to make our appearance more intoxicating, before sashaying to the entrance.

"Welcome to Cuban Ice, ladies. How may I make your life easier today?" an overweight Cuban with a receding hairline greeted us in his broken English after pushing the button on his shirt pocket to buzz us in. I eyed Passion with the quickness, motioning to her to show the man some compassion, while I made my way to the back because we knew this definitely wasn't Gio.

"What did you have in mind, Papi?" I heard Passion seductively ask while walking towards him behind the counter. I pretended I was browsing all the fine pieces of jewelry they had to offer, until I had the chance to make my way to the back without being noticed. That proved to be easier said than done. Every time I thought I had him fooled, I looked up and his fat ass would be staring right at me. *Damn*, I thought as I made my way to join the party. While Passion sat on his lap giving him a perfect view of her thirty-six double-D breasts, I went between his legs, unbuttoned his slacks and then swiftly pulled out his too-small dick. Hard as it was, I suppressed the urge to laugh in his face, before making do with what he was working with as I slowly stroked him to an erection. I stroked and stroked until I heard moans of pleasure, and as his breathing became heavier, I slowly tapped Passion to get her attention.

Once she looked over her shoulder at me, I looked at his dick and then back at her, giving her the signal to give him some of that golden head everybody say she had. She did a double-take once she saw how small his dick was and then looked back at me with wide eyes, while shaking her head no.

I swear I wanted to kick her in her ass right then and there because she knew our motto, "do whatever you have to do to get the job done," so somebody please tell me why was this bitch acting like a fuckin nun. I looked at her again, this time to let her know she needed to kill the bullshit and handle her business.

She rolled her eyes before puttin her finger in her mouth, signaling that she wanted to throw up, but slowly rose to her feet and stood in between his legs. I continued to stroke until her lips were just inches away from his dick, but the minute her tongue wrapped around its head and his eyes closed, I was on my way to find Gio.

I slowly walked the dark hallway with the right side of my dress slightly pulled up, so I would have easy access to my burna in case I needed it. I didn't know what to expect as I tried every door in my path to see what was behind it while at the same time ready to kill or be killed. Altogether, I counted four doors, two on each side and every one of them I found empty until I reached the last one on the right. I put my ear to the door and could hear faint moans from a man and a woman. They spoke Spanish to each other and even though I could understand nothing they said, I still found myself trying to break down bits and pieces of their conversation.

Finally, not wanting to waste any more time, I pulled my burna all the way out and counted to three in my head before slowly easing the door open. The lights were off, but I could hear the voices louder now than I did before, as I rubbed my hand across the wall in search of the light switch. The moment the darkened room was filled with light, I automatically recognized Gio between the spread legs of a Spanish girl, who looked as if she could be no older then sixteen or seventeen.

I aimed my burna back and forth at the them as I continued to stare and could literally feel myself getting moist between my own legs. Sex was the last thing on my mind though, what turned me on so much was the sight of all the blue-face, hundred-dollar bills they were fucking on. Yeah, there was so much money, you could barely see the bed underneath them.

Without a second thought, I walked up to Gio and smashed the butt of my burna into his face, before warning the girl that I'd kill her if she screamed. She quickly covered her mouth and her private parts as the tears started down her face. Gio continued to lay on the floor with both hands over his face, trying to stop the blood that poured out like a faucet, while yelling I picked the wrong Cuban to fuck with.

"Get that pillow and cover his face with it," I told the girl as I watched and waited. She hesitated at first, but quickly caught my drift when I raised my burna to her head. Once I heard the muffled screams that have gotten louder than before, I pushed my burna into the pillow and let off three shots, stopping all sounds and move-ment. The girl continued to cover her mouth, this time not feeling shy about her nakedness as a scream threatened to escape her lips.

"Listen, bitch, what you're about to do now is go get that pillow off the bed, remove the pillowcase and then fill it with every bill you see. Do you understand me?" I said in a more demanding tone after getting tired of watching how spooked the bitch was. This time she shook her head, indicating she understood, before scooping up the money like a stripper who had just turned the club up with her performance.

"Please don't kill me, I'm only seventeen," she begged once she finished filling the second pillowcase with the money that fell on the floor. I wanted to spare her life with every inch of my soul, because she reminded me so much of Passion's little sister, but the bitch was in the wrong place at the wrong time. In this line of work, you could never leave any witnesses, unless you wanted them to come back one day and get revenge.

"Put your clothes on, you're coming with me," I stated, ignoring the pleas to spare her life. While she got dressed, I noticed for the first time that the TV screen next to the bed showed video footage of the security cameras around the store. I quickly stopped it from recording and then took the DVD, before forcing the girl to pick up both pillowcases. With her leading the way, I kept my burna pressed in the lower part of her back as we moved to the entrance of the store.

The minute we stepped through the door that separated the front from the back, I witnessed for the second time tonight a bitch naked from the waist down, with her legs spread wide open for the world to see. The only different this time was instead of getting dicked down, Passion was letting this fat muthafucka eat her pussy. I wasted no time showing my anger as I shot him two times in the back and then once in the head. When his body hit the floor, Passion jumped up angry, I guess because she didn't get the nut she was looking for. But fuck the bullshit, it was time to get the fuck out of here.

She squeezed back into her jeans as I grabbed both pillowcases from the girl before making her stand in the corner with her back to us. Passion looked at me confused, but bad as I didn't want to do it, I gave her the head nod and without a second thought, Passion shot her two times in the head.

I did the best I could not to show any emotions. How I was raised, emotions will get you killed, but she didn't deserve it she was still a baby. I quickly brushed the thought out my head before

Passion sensed something was bothering me and headed towards the door.

"Champagne!" Passion called, trying to get my attention but I kept walking. I mean, I heard her, but I didn't hear her if that makes any sense. My mind was just somewhere else. I grabbed the door handle to leave and the craziest thing happened, the muthafucka wouldn't open.

"Bitch, that's what I was trying to tell you, the man got the fuckin button on his shirt pocket to open the door," she said, making me feel dumb as hell. I waited patiently for her to push the god damn button like rush hour and once she did, we were out the door and to the car in record time.

The next morning, I called Mahogany to let her know how everything went. She tooted a bitch's horn, bragging about how she knew Passion and I would handle our business.

"Y'all might want to go celebrate, because y'all just put in work for a very important and a very wealthy man. I can't say his name, but trust me he knows who you are," Mahogany said, before whispering a little secret in my ear before hanging up. I thought hard about what she just told me and to be honest, I couldn't wait.

"Champagne! Champagne! Bitch, guess who's performing at Eight Seconds tonight?" Passion yelled like I couldn't hear her if she used her inside voice. And she wondered why I ignore her loudmouth ass all the time. I looked at her like she was crazy once she appeared in my room and stood in front of me.

"Bitch, NBA YoungBoy and yo boo Plies. Now, you know we gotta slide through and ball out like real Baller Babies." The minute she started talking about balling, it reminded me that we still hadn't counted the money in the two pillowcases we got from the jewelry store last night. I rushed to my closet, leaving her looking more confused than a virgin boy about to receive his first piece of pussy.

"Count this!" I told her once I returned and threw her one of the pillowcases. An hour and a half later, we both lay on the floor tired and exhausted, a half a million dollars lay next to us.

"What's the plan, we going to Eight Seconds tonight or what?" Passion asked with her eye lids barely open. I thought about it for a second and then looked at the money, I mean Mahogany did tell us to go out and celebrate. Do you know what I can do with two hundred and fifty thousand dollars, damn right we going out tonight I thought to myself.

"Say less, bitch, tonight is ours and we're about to ball like we invented sports," I said, before hittin her in the face with a stack of bills that still had another bitch's pussy scent on it. She threw one back and then next thing I know, we were taking a money shower.

Night fell and Passion and I both rapped to NBA YoungBoy's "Outside Today," as we cruised University Avenue on our way to Eight Seconds. I can't deny it, a bitch did feel happy I came out, instead of staying cooped up in the house. It looked as if the whole city was out tonight as I looked around and saw all the tricked-out Chevy's, Maxima's and Infiniti's. I was thinking about dropping some rims on my Beemer, but I really didn't know, I still hadn't made up my mind yet.

"Where the hell we gone park at?" Passion asked when she saw every parking space was filled once we turned into Eight Seconds' lot. I looked around and couldn't believe it my damn self, there really wasn't anywhere to park. I made a U-turn, driving across the street and catching a spot right as a car was leaving.

"About fuckin time!" Passion shouted as we both got out the car and sashayed across the street, causing a traffic jam on the way. Yeah, you heard me right, I said we were stopping fuckin traffic. I was killing the game in my high-slit, two-toned, custom made dress by David Koma. My hair laid in curls on my shoulders, while my Prada clutch bag held nothing but big faces.

Passion loved the attention more so than I did and that's just what she got as she turned heads in her Gucci mini skirt, white leather Gucci jacket and her Stuart Weitzman pumps. Her naturally curly hair fell loosely down her back, while her make-up-free face showed just a hint of clear lip gloss.

We stood in front of Eight Seconds and couldn't believe how long the line was. Well, let me take that back. I could believe it, because Eight Seconds was the club you wanted to be at. The parking lot itself was so big, it was like a club outside a club, but you wanted to be inside because it was literally in the sky. It was on the rooftop of this skyscraper-like building, but at the same time, it had a roof held up by stainless steel poles and burglar bars surrounding it to keep people from falling to the ground.

"Girl, how long you been waiting out here?" I asked a random chick who stood in line, because I was contemplating what I wanted to do.

"Two damn hours and this shit don't make no fuckin sense," she replied, looking like she was getting mad just from thinking about it. I knew right then waiting in line was not something I was about to do, so Passion and I both walked up to the door.

"I need to holla at the owner, the manager or whoever running this bitch tonight," I said with a no-bullshit attitude. The bouncer laughed at me but went to get the man in charge anyway. I sized him up as he did the same to me, but before he could say anything, I pulled out twenty thousand dollars and pushed the stack of bills to his chest.

"Enough said, that's twenty racks of free bands. Me and my girl cashing in on the whole club for the night, so that means everybody out here getting in this bitch for free, compliments of the Baller Babies."

With that being said, we walked up the staircase as the whole line followed and screamed out, "Baller Babies," which hyped us up even more.

"Tryna hide from cameras. Ain't goin outside today!" I sang along as soon as I stepped foot in the door and turned up when the neon lights went to changing colors. I couldn't believe it. *I'm really in this bitch with Plies and NBA YoungBoy*, I thought as I started dancing. They performed and mingled in the VIP section, something I've never seen before.

"Come on, girl, I'm about to go ask Plies and YoungBoy to come to the photo booth with us to take some pictures," Passion said excitedly, while trying to pull me with her.

"Hell no, girl!" I replied, snatching my hand back. "You go by yourself and come get me if they say yes."

I didn't think she would really ask, but she did and to my surprise, they told her yes. Knowing Passion, she probably wouldn't take no for an answer anyway. She rushed to me, grabbing my hand like she did before, only this time I went with her. We introduced ourselves with them doing the same, which I didn't know why, because the whole world already knew who they were.

"Y'all ready?" the man taking the picture asked and I could tell he was getting impatient, so just to piss him off a little more, I threw two thousand dollars at him and told him to snap until he ran out of space in his camera, while we acted a fool in the booth. We took over fifty pictures and once I gave Plies a hug and a kiss on the cheek, he and YoungBoy hit the stage for their last performance.

"Before we do these last songs, I wanna give a shout out the Baller Babies. Y'all showed us that Gainesville really be cutting up. This here for y'all, compliments of ya lil whoa, Plies," Plies said, before his hit song blasted over the speakers and I can't lie, the whole fuckin city heard us that night.

"Let me think tonight what I'mma do at the club, I might show up tonight just to throw dubs, or I might buy the bar out to fuck with the scrub, how I feel tonight shawty, I am the club!" we rapped as I danced my way to the window overlooking the parking lot, with Passion right on my heel. This was a night I wanted everybody out here to remember for many years to come, and it was only one way to make that happen.

While Plies was finishing up his song and motivating us at the same time, Passion and I both grabbed stacks out of our handbags and made it rain on everybody outside the window parking lot pimpin. Real boss shit, Double B's, bitch!

Keith Williams

Chapter 4

CoCo

I sat in my room and smoked Loud pack after Loud pack, as I took my mind through a mental roller coaster, thinking about how I was gone get my revenge. I was waiting to see if E'mani beat the murder charge or not, because I couldn't let this shit blow away like the wind, she gotta get it. Mahogany too for that matter, because I know she either set my sister up or she knew about what was going down. That's the real reason I moved back to Panama City with my mother. I didn't know who to trust anymore and now that my sister was gone, I'll be damned if I let a bitch trick me out of my life.

I picked up a photo of me, Shanel, Nah Nah, Nicole, Kayla and Mahogany. We were all graduating from the Florida Institution for Teenage Girls and we took a group picture in our cap and gowns. It's crazy out of all six of us, four are now dead, and it's now smoke between the last two. I laughed, because back then I would've never thought things would end like this, we were the fuckin Baller Babies.

I started reminiscing about the time Shanel's boyfriend Trey, sent his god sister Kara to visit her with an ounce of Molly in her pussy. I was scared as hell for Shanel because she had never done anything like that before, but she made it back safe, thank God.

The moment she did, the Crips ran into her room with knifes and combination locks wrapped around socks. They forced Shanel down, stripped her naked and went between her legs, taking everything. I ran in there after them intending to help my sister, but I was quickly forced to the wall with a knife held to my throat. I can't lie I was scared as hell but then here came Mahogany, a girl we didn't even know at the time, with about ten girls behind her.

They turned my sister's room into a crime scene, I mean, there was blood everywhere. I grabbed Shanel's hand and got out of there fast as I could. She was still naked and all, but we made it, until the C.O. stopped us.

Two months later when we all got out of confinement, Mahogany stepped to Shanel and me with a business proposition, not even mentioning what happened with the Crips. I was wondering if there was still smoke, but at the same time I was a little confused, because before the Crips ran into Shanel's room, I saw Mahogany talking and laughing with them same girls, but really didn't pay it no attention.

Back in my room, I was high as hell as I continued to smoke and think everything through. I shook my head and laughed because back then I was naive as hell, but now that I think about it, it was Mahogany that sent them girls at Shanel, before coming to help us like she was doing us a favor to get in on our hustle. She finessed us all the way around the board, just like she probably finessed E'mani to actually pull the trigger on Shanel and was finessing me now, acting like she didn't have anything to do with my sister's death.

"I swear to God, sis, everybody who had something to do with your murder gone die, I promise you that or I'll be seeing you real soon," I promised Shanel, meaning every word as I tore the picture I held into tiny pieces, because in my eyes the Baller Babies were dead. I stumbled to my feet and then looked around, not knowing what the hell I was actually looking for. *I'm going fuckin crazy*, I thought as I rubbed my hand all over my body, feeling a cold chill tackle me.

"Damn, that felt good," I moaned when I brushed across my sensitive nipples. I touched them again before pinching them and felt the moisture between my legs. I don't know what it is about weed, but it makes you horny as hell. My whole body felt so fuckin sensitive. I stripped out of all my clothes while making my way to my dresser to retrieve my vibrator.

Lately, besides smoking Loud, fulfilling my sexual desire has been my therapy. I turned my bullet on high and slowly brought it to my nipples as I closed my eyes and fantasized about my last golden head. I fantasized about how he always ran his tongue across each of my hardened nipples, before softly biting them between his teeth. I moaned to him how good the pain, felt while slightly pushing his head further south.

"Eat me, baby," I continued to moan as he tongued my navel, teasing me on his way down. I wanted to cum just from the feeling of his hot breath on my skin. My own breathing became shallow as I anticipated his skillful tongue boxing my clit, and then I felt it. The rotation of his tongue up, down and around my clit was driving me insane, before he pushed it deep inside my pussy lips, reaching my sweet candy. I inhaled deeply before exhaling again, revealing the initial shock of the much-needed pleasure I was receiving.

"Make me cum, please make me cum," I begged, pushing his face deeper and deeper into my pussy. I wasn't hard to please, but I purposely held back while encouraging him, so it would intensify the waves of my orgasm. With each lick of his tongue, he brought me closer to reaching my peak. I wanted it so bad that my legs started to shake and the minute he found my G-spot, it felt as if I was releasing my soul through my pussy as I came all over his face and in his mouth.

Once I opened my eyes, which I had to adjust to the sunlight shining through the window, there he was in the flesh. My next-door neighbor T-man, the golden head, the man I was just fantasizing about. I quickly got over the initial shock and lashed out, not caring that I was completely naked while my vibrator still hummed in my hand.

"You called me," he responded as I watched him stare at my pussy through my spread legs. I was confused, not knowing what the hell he was talking about and before I could tell him, he stopped me.

"CoCo, I know your moans from anywhere and besides, I see you need a hand, or should I say a tongue and a dick."

Once he saw that he brought a smile to my face, he quickly stripped out of his clothes before slowly stroking his dick to a full erection. I wanted it. I can't lie, I mean, I wanted it with every horny bone in my body and he wasn't gone deprive me of it by teasing me. I reached out and grabbed hold of him, not being able to wait any longer, and pulled him to me before swallowing every last inch.

Yeah, I was a real maneater and on my way to becoming a golden head. I spit on it, softly bit on it and then spit on it some more, because I knew he loved to receive sloppy head, and I liked to give it even more. We stared each other in the eyes while I made his dick disappear then reappear like magic, but before I knew it, I was on my back with my legs wrapped around his waist.

"Oh, shit! T-man, make it hurt, go deeper. I want it." I tried holding back because I saw he was trying to make love and I wanted to be pounded. He quickly caught on as time passed and took control by flipping me over to eat my pussy from behind. I continued to push my ass back forcing him deeper, while he pulled my hair to let me know how good this pussy was.

Moments like this, who needed words when you had dick like this, and this dick was forcing me to cum all over it. He pushed me to the edge of the bed with my hands now palming the floor, and before I had a chance to prepare myself for it, he was sending me to the moon by slapping his dick all over this juicy pussy and causing me to squirt like never before.

Once I calmed down and my breathing went back to normal, I thanked T-man before handing him a fifty-dollar bill and sending him home. He complained like always, but took the money anyway, claimed I make him feel like a trick the way I paid him every time we fucked. I laughed because that's just what he was. I hated it when a person feelings got involved. I mean, from the jump, we both knew what we were getting into.

I was now exhausted and just wanted to be dead to the world for a couple hours. Sorry to say a couple hours turned out to be forty-five minutes, because I was quickly awakened by my growling stomach.

"Ma!" I yelled but got no response. I yelled again and the house still sounded like nothing, so I jumped out of bed and quickly got dressed. *I know Mama's not back to smoking that damn crack again,* I thought as I was headed to the living room. The last time I had that feeling I was right, but I swear, I'll kill her ass my damn self if she relapsed. "Ma!" I continued to yell and for the third time got no reply.

Now I was starting to worry and wanted to know what the hell was going on, until I walked in the kitchen and read the note she left on the counter. She was letting me know that she went to her yoga class for couples and I would have to go out to eat because she didn't cook.

"Couples?" I laughed because I didn't know what the hell Mama was doing there. The whole world knew she didn't have a man. I hated the fact that she didn't cook though, because now I had to really get all dressed up before going outside. I took a quick shower before re-curling my hair and throwing on my Chanel sundress and silver pumps. Damn, when I viewed the name on the dress, it just made me think about my sister. I continued getting ready, now applying my eyeliner, because I promised myself, I wasn't gone cry anymore. Shanel wouldn't want that anyway. I know she would be cursing my ass out for doing all that damn crying. Once I was diva ready, I grabbed my keys and sashayed to my Dodge Charger before throwing on my RayBan Shades.

I tried to beat the happy hour traffic as I swiftly avoided the main streets and thought about the Freaky Friday topic, Angela Yee from The Breakfast Club on 93.3 The Beat, asked the world to comment on. "If you had to choose between having sex every night with a terrible lover, or having sex once a year with an amazing lover, which would be your cup of tea?"

I listened and laughed at the men and women across the world explaining how they would have to deal with the terrible sex every night, because once a year is too damn long to wait to get that itch scratched. Me, on the other hand… yeah, I'll agree with everybody about not waiting a whole year to get some dick. But at the same time, I am not letting a nigga with no fuck game get on top of me and fuck me every night either. I don't have a problem with being a teacher every once in a while and showing him what I like and how to please me.

I got caught at a stop light about a block away from Golden Corral, where I planned to eat, and it seemed as if the muthafucka would never turn green. I waited and waited seriously contemplating on turning my ass around and going another way, but it was too many cars blocking me off. Ten minutes into the wait, the light finally switched to green, and I couldn't tell you how happy I was to get closer to my destination. I turned into the parking lot of Golden Corral and was almost side swiped by three teenagers in a black Chevy Malibu, driving like they just stole the muthafucka.

"Y'all need to watch where the fuck y'all going!" I yelled as I tapped my horn like a mad woman. Kids these days just don't have no damn respect and then on top of that, all you see on the news are kids with guns running around shooting their damn schools up, that's a shame they ain't got no damn home training. I parked after searching the parking lot for a spot and then stepped out. There wasn't any cameras around but I damn sure sashayed towards the entrance of the restaurant like I was Naomi Campbell. It was just a habit I couldn't break… yeah, a bad bitch habit.

"Welcome to Golden Corral," the pretty blonde girl at the cash register greeted me. I smiled back before paying the eatery fee, grabbing my tray and going on my way. I hated being rude, but I had the munchies like a muthafucka, so conversation was not something I wanted to be holding right now. I stacked my tray as if I was feeding a small village, knowing damn well I wasn't about to eat it all but who's to stop me from trying. I was one of them small petite females that didn't get fat. No matter what I ate, my figure always stayed on point and I didn't even work out.

Once I started to eat, I threw down like a nigga out the pen. Fuck trying to be all ladylike, I was hungry. Fried chicken, macaroni and cheese, rice and beans, and chocolate-covered strawberries for dessert, yeah all that. I was doing it big for all my bitches that's still locked down doing time in the Florida Institution for Teenage Girls, free all my real bitches.

While I was stuffing my face, for the life of me, I couldn't ignore the little boy throwing a temper tantrum, while his mother looked as if she was trying her best not to show her ass in these white folks' place of business. The little boy cried while I stared, trying to figure out who it was he reminded me of, but it wouldn't come to me.

"Jermaine! Boy, if you don't close your mouth, I swear I'll leave you right here so these white folks can have you," the lady said through clenched teeth. I looked once more and then who the little boy reminded me of hit me, but I didn't understand how it could be, all the way up here in Panama City.

"Excuse me, I don't mean to get in your business, but do you mind if he has this?" I asked as I handed the little boy my stress ball to play with. Before she had a chance to say anything the crying stopped, and his attention was on the ball.

"Thank you so much because he was really starting to get on my last damn nerve," she responded as we both laughed. "By the way, my name is Daniesse."

I shook her hand and introduced myself but couldn't stop myself from admiring her five-two frame and long, straight, black shoulder-length hair that she let hang down and framed her face. Her almond-shaped eyes revealed a hint of her life, but I was hoping she would be willing to break it all down to me in the future, no lesbian shit.

Keith Williams

Chapter 5

Mahogany

"Mahogany! Girl, you need to sit your ass down, fuck that bitch we can handle this ourselves," Champagne said as she grabbed my arm, stopping me from walking a hole in the carpet.

I called CoCo one last time and got no answer, before throwing my phone out of frustration. It was finally time to handle the business I said would make the world remember us until they're dead and gone, and even their kids will talk about us. And this bitch CoCo wasn't answering her phone. That was strike-one for her ass. Yeah, I understood she was grieving over her sister, but so am I. She needed to stop acting like a fuckin child and get her shit together.

"Fuck it, let's go, we ain't got that much time anyway," I told Champagne as we headed to the car. I had been working on this plan for about two months now and I couldn't believe how well it was coming together.

Ashlyn and Alice's father was a real wealthy man by the name of Lester Wright. He started off investing in the stock market as a side hustle and having an eye for these kind of things, he quickly made a fortune. He trusted nobody because of his profession and the decisions he made that ruined peoples' lives, so the security system on his multimillion-dollar home was like something you'd expect to see at the White House.

But like all men, pussy was his downfall. I found out that he had a thing for young red bitches so I sent Passion to fulfill his every need like a playmate to get us access to his home and it paid off, because one thing my bitches knew how to do was run circles around a nigga's ass. I read the address given to me by Michael Conn to Alexa and the bitch acted as if she didn't know what the hell I was talking about. That's the thing about these electronics, they never do what they were supposed to do.

"Hold up, Mahogany, hold up. Let me talk to her, because you don't know how to talk to a bitch," Champagne told me as she cleared her throat. I looked at her like she was fuckin crazy, because she was. What the hell she mean, I don't know how to talk to a bitch? This was a damn cell phone, how else am I supposed to talk to the muthafucka?

She read the address to Alexa and like magic, the bitch gave us directions. I smiled to keep from getting frustrated, because Champagne showed no sympathy as she rubbed it in my face that she was right. After a couple minutes and a long ass dirty roads, we finally made it.

"What now?" Champagne asked as we sat in the car and watched the movement of this compound-like home. Everything looked quiet, there was no movement, no men guarding the house nor were there any dogs running around that I saw. But, Passion told me to be on point at all times when we got there, because Lester was paranoid and you just never knew how he was thinking.

"This what we gone do." I started as we continued looking around. "We going in through the back of the house, which Passion said she would have unlocked for us, but we have to get by the security cameras he got around the property." Champagne looked out the window with a stale face and I could tell she wanted to say something, so I asked.

She waved me off saying, "Nothing," but I know her, she wasn't the type to bite her tongue.

"What's on your mind, you looking all crazy and shit, what you got to say?"

She continued to say, "Nothing," but now she was looking at me. I stared back and finally she broke. "Fuck that, I hate your plan. I say we go to the front door, ring the doorbell and when he answer it, he get to meet the barrel of my nine." She smiled as if her plan was worth a million dollars and she was the only one who could've thought of it.

"Bitch, you sound stupid, the element of surprise is a muthafucka. Now why would we let him know we're out here if we don't have to? Think bitch, think!" I shot back, wondering if she knew how dumb she sounded. I mean, my intentions wasn't to go off on her, but sometimes you just have to think before you open your mouth, because Mahogany don't like the smell of shit, I mean, bull-shit all the time.

We went with my plan after going back and forth with each other for a little while and then got out the car. I led the way as we stayed close to the house so we wouldn't be caught by the cameras, but still no signs of guards or dogs, so we continued and made it to the back of the house where we entered.

"Listen, Champagne, now that we're here, let's not get into that back and forth arguing shit anymore because we need to stay fo-cused and take care of this business, you agree?" I said, looking into her eyes once the door closed. She agreed with no slick remarks and then gave me a hug before we started up the stairs. On my left, I saw movement out of my peripheral vision as we got closer to the door, which was ajar. Once I peeped in to see there was only one person there, we both rushed her with the barrels of our guns damn near touching the tip of her nose.

"If you scream, I swear I will blow your fuckin face off, do you understand me?" I demanded before she had a chance to do any-thing. She shook her head up and down, indicating she understood, and I continued with the questions.

"Now, who are you and how many more people are here in this house with you? And I dare you to lie to me." She hesitated as if she thought about the consequences of lying to me, before breaking down like a beat-up Chevy.

"Please don't kill me! My name is Ashlyn, my sister Alice is in her room next door, and my dad is in his room with his girlfriend three doors down. There is nobody else in the house, I promise, please don't hurt me and my family. We have money if that's what you want."

I stared at her with my face balled up and the first thing came to mind were the two names. E'mani mouthed to me the day the police took her. Ashlyn and Alice? How were they out of jail and E'mani was still there awaiting trial. They had my bitch fucked all the way up, something foul was going on and I was about to find out. I sent Champagne to go get Alice while I stayed with Ashlyn, hoping the bitch would act stupid, so I could leave her ass with a hole in the middle of her fuckin face.

"Why are you and your sister out of jail and E'mani still there waiting to go to trial so you can testify against her?" I asked as I stared a hole in her face. She cried and shook her head as if she didn't want to answer me but the sight of my .45 will make anybody get right.

"This is bigger than Alice and I, and even bigger than Daddy. The Baller Babies fucked over my older sister and she won't stop until they're all dead," she spoke with volume. "She's mad about Ja'mya and even madder about Supreme and we can't stop her now."

Damn, so this shit is still about Supreme, it's like a bad dream I can't wake up from. Also, who the hell is her older sister and what the hell she has to do with Supreme? I thought as my mind started racing. "Who the fuck is this older sister you're talking about?" I yelled, now pissed the fuck off. This bitch was playing with my fuckin emotions and I didn't like it. So, I damn near forced the barrel of my gun inside her eye socket. "Tell me who the fuck is it!"

"Mahogany, hold on, don't shoot her yet. We still have to make sure Passion is safe," Champagne yelled to me as she stood there with her gun aimed at the person, I assumed to be Alice. I looked back and forth from Ashlyn to Alice, hating the sight of snitching ass bitches and wanted to end their life right there, but Champagne was right. I was contemplating on telling Champagne about the Baller Babies still being on top of somebody's hit list, but at the same time, I wanted to get more info before I broke it down to her.

"Let's go, take us to Daddy's room, he should enjoy the surprise it's to die for," I joked as they led the way and Champagne and I followed. I kept my gun aimed at them both, expecting the worse when we got there. But the minute the door was opened, all we saw was a naked Lester with both his arms and legs tied to the bed post as Passion rode him cowgirl style with no hands.

We all stared watching as Passion showed off one of her many talents with neither her nor Lester knowing they had acquired an audience. She rocked her hips and rubbed her clit as she raised herself, so his dick were just inches away from slipping out of her glistening pussy. Without missing a beat, she gripped the head with her vagina muscles until he warned her he was about to cum, before she slid back down, riding the waves of her own orgasm as she threw her head back in bliss.

Ashlyn and Alice both looked as if they wanted to vomit, watching their dad having sex, but at no time did they turn their heads from the performance. Without warning, I gave them both a round of applause for the wonderful show they put together for us tonight.

"Brilliant, that was so brilliant. Passion you should get an Oscar, because that looked so damn real," I said as Passion and Lester both looked at us surprised. Lester looked more embarrassed then surprised and I'm pretty sure it had everything to do with his daughters seeing him tied up while Passion had her way with him.

"Crystal, what's going on?" Lester asked Passion, using the alias she gave him as she started putting her clothes back on. She didn't answer and once I handed her the .25 I had tucked in the back of my pants, it was all self-explanatory.

"Now, since all parties are present, I would like to know how the hell the two of you got out of jail while E'mani is still there awaiting trial?" I asked, breaking the silence. Both girls just looked at each other as if to say they wasn't going to be the one to tell.

"Okay, so nobody wants to talk, I can fix that real fast." Before I could get to the bed to their father, Ashlyn spoke up.

"Please, whatever we did, we're sorry. I told you before, the only reason we're out is because my sister is a very powerful person. We told her E'mani and the Baller Babies hired us to give Supreme HIV, but in order for her to arrest E'mani, we had to do a week in jail, so nothing seemed suspicious and then—"

"Ashlyn, shut your mouth right now!" their father shouted aggressively. Champagne, Passion and I all looked around wondering the same thing. Well, the way they were looking I figured they were thinking what I was thinking. Who the hell is this older sister they're talking about and how much power does this bitch really have?

"Fuck the bullshit, this is how it's going down. Since your family wants the Baller Babies dead, I'm changing the plan. We came here on behalf of E'mani to get your father to convince you two bitches to change your mind about testifying, but now you all have to die. Passion, Champagne!" I said and without further explanation, we shot every last one of them in the head, ignoring their protests.

Passion then ran to the bathroom but returned two minutes later, with a container filled with soap and water. Champagne and I both watched, wondering what the hell she was doing but the minute she walked towards the bed, everything became clear to me. She was doing what any smart bitch in her right mind would do to keep her damn freedom, wiping Lester's body clean of any DNA she was sure she left on him.

My bitches sometimes surprised me when it came to having knowledge of the streets, but I guess going through so much in life forces you into situations you wouldn't normally be in, causing you to learn from your past.

"Snap out of it, bitch, we got work to do," Passion stated, bringing me back to the present as I stood there like a zombie. Once we searched the house and found the security footage, we wiped down everything we touched before setting the whole house on fire, hoping the security system wouldn't alert the fire department before the bitch burned down. Yeah, I know I was making this shit a habit, killing people and then setting the whole building on fire. Once Doe Boy became my first victim, I've been turned out ever since, but this one was for a good cause.

For those of you that don't know, here's a little history on us. The Baller Babies wasn't started because we liked robbing and killing bitches, to be honest, that was far from the reason. We were just six real ass bitches trying to get paid out of a fucked-up situation because think about it who didn't want to be the number-one stunna like Birdman.

Once we got back to the city limits of St. Petersburg, we were turned up like the volume on a Benz, the way we were hanging out.

We had a blunt of Loud in rotation and we were all screaming, "YOLO," like we knew the world was about to end.

I laughed as I controlled the wheel, but Champagne and Passion were really reminding me of my fallin bitches, especially Champagne. The way she was always on go, she was like Nah Nah and Nicole together, and we all knew that was a hell of a combination. I couldn't really compare Passion, but if I had to, I would say she was a Shanel the way she didn't mind puttin in work. But on the other hand, the white girl in her came out every once in a while, like E'mani.

"What's poppin, boo?" I yelled out the window to the brown-skinned brother with the pretty white teeth who was pushing a black Mustang. He smiled back but threw up the deuces like I was some damn groupie.

"Girl, I know he ain't just dis you like you was some bum ass bitch? He can't have no idea who you are," Champagne stated as I swerved in his lane and followed him. I have never had a man not want me when I was trying to give him a chance and I can't lie, that shit was fucking with a bitch's ego. I followed him a short distance to MLK Park, the one I drove to last week and got stupid high, while Ice Billion Berg rapped exactly how I felt to the world.

He jumped out of his car first and just sat on the hood watching as Champagne, Passion and I exited the car like the world was ours.

"I guess you must really like what you—" Before he could finish his sentence, I put my finger to his lips stopping whatever he planned to say and illustrated on his ass like E'mani would say.

"I chase no man, so never get it twisted. I'm a bad bitch from the top of my head to the bottom of my feet. I get my own coins, so confuse me not with the bum ass bitches I guess you so used to dealing with. Yeah, I like what I see but the only thing a man got for me is a hard dick, some golden head and loyalty. Nothing more, nothing less."

He sized me up with a smirk on his face before apologizing for disrespecting me. Like any man he got his mind right, realizing he had a real bitch in his presence.

"Again, I apologize. There was no harm intended on my end, but you have to understand being a man of my caliber, gold diggin women throw themselves at me all the time. I prefer we just start over though. I'm Ruger, but my friend calls me Rue for short and you?" he said, extending his hand to me. I laughed but introduced myself and shook his hand anyway.

It was just crazy the way everything played out, he dissed a bitch at first and now he wants to start over, getting to know me after I put him in his place. Yeah, I call that the bad bitch "trick-a-nigga" spell. I introduced Champagne and Passion to Rue before we exchanged cell phone numbers then parted ways.

"Pass the Loud, bitch, we tryna get high like palm trees to before we get back on the road and head home!" Passion yelled over the music as we turned back up, feeling like teenagers who just got a new car for our birthday. I loved my bitches and not just Champagne and Passion, I mean all my bitches dead and alive. Once we got to my house, I gave them both a hug and told them to be safe before sending them home.

"Home sweet home!" I shouted soon as my feet touched the plush carpet. I was tired as ever, but I took me a quick shower before calling it a night. Ten minutes into my dream, I found myself waking up to call CoCo again, and just like before the bitch still didn't answer.

Chapter 6

E'mani

"I'm Brittany Collins and if you're just tuning in, I'm bringing you the latest from the suburban area house fire in St. Petersburg. It has been revealed that three bodies have been found, and the cause of death seems to be a single gunshot to the head before the house was set on fire. No arrests have been made in connection to this case, but we've learned the three bodies have been identified as Circuit Judge Lester Wright and his two daughters, Ashlyn and Alice Wright.

"No motive has been revealed as of yet and besides the St. Petersburg massacre almost two months ago, this has been the biggest tragedy in the beautiful sunshine state of Florida. Ladies and gentlemen, that's all the news I have for now, but we will be sure to bring you the updates as they come to us. So, stay tuned and remember, you heard it here first. I'm Brittany Collins, and this is C.F.T.N.S."

It felt like my ass had been glued to the chair as I wouldn't get up from my spot even after the news went off. I couldn't get what Brittany Collins said out of my head. How the hell did Ashlyn and Alice get out of jail for a bitch to be able to kill them? I didn't know if I should be happy and jump up and down or worry about what's next to come. There was a big chance I could be getting out any day now, but there also was a chance I could be escorted to booking, facing new charges.

This mess had Mahogany's name written all over it but I gave her my word I would trust her, so I had no choice but to ride it out. I went to my room after about ten minutes, dropped to my knees and just poured my heart out to God. I prayed and prayed, not just for me but for Mahogany, the Baller Babies, my mother and even for Ashlyn, Alice and their family. I didn't know what else to do, so I went to sleep praying this was all a bad dream, and I would wake up in my bed and illustrate on Mahogany for playing her music too damn loud.

"Newman, you have an attorney visit so get ready, I'll be back in ten minutes." An officer I've never seen woke me up. Once I did get out of my bed, I relieved my bladder and then washed my hands, before brushing my teeth. I was kind of happy Michael Conn was here to see me, because I needed to talk to him ASAP. My jury selection was only two days away and I wanted to know where we stood.

I was placed in handcuffs through the bars and then let out, with the officer walking behind me and again, I threw some extra sway in my hips to see his reaction. He stared like I knew he would, but instead of grabbing his dick as he fantasized, he repeatedly licked his thick lips. I knew he truly couldn't help it. My petite, five-foot-two frame, light-skinned complexion and Cardi B-type ass was like a magnet to any man. They just couldn't resist it.

The minute we turned the corner, I spotted Michael Conn as he waited for them to escort me in, with a stern "no bullshit" look on his face. I wasn't a psychic, so I had no idea what was on his mind, but after all the shit I've been through since I been here, he better have something good to tell me.

"Good evening, Ms. Newman, I'm pretty sure you've been watching the news lately, so I won't get into details, but I will say this. I fully intend to talk with the prosecutor before jury selection about dropping these bogus charges," he said the second the officer was out of earshot.

I smiled for the first time today, because it gave me hope to hear him say that. He went on to explain the steps we would have to take to get me out of this hell hole and I was pleased to know Plies was right when he said, "Money talk and bullshit walk a thousand miles."

"Just try and relax and stay stress free, because I'm positive you'll be out of here, give me one week, max. Oh yeah, and before I forget, Mahogany and the Baller Babies sent their love."

Once he started packing up his paperwork, I sat and waited on the officer, feeling like a proud parent because Mahogany had just sent proof of what I had already figured. Yeah, she's the mastermind behind the murder and arson of the suburban home here in St. Petersburg and she sent her love to let me know it. Damn, my bitch always had my back that's why our bond could never be broken. I openly flirted with the male officer who escorted me, as his pretty boy features made me moist. I purposely stopped in front of him, causing him to walk into me, putting his dick and his chest all over my ass and back.

"Excuse me, shawty, that was my fault. You alright?" He apologized, making sure I wasn't hurt as I turned to face him. I stared him in the eyes seductively as I smiled and shook my head yes, giving him the sign that I liked what I felt.

"Shawty, you gone make me lose my job you keep looking at me like that." Catching the hidden message that he also liked what I had to offer, I pushed my ass into his hand and encouraged him to feel how soft it was, as he gave it a firm squeeze. I couldn't stop the soft moans as they escaped my lips, being that I haven't had a man touch me like that in so long.

"Shawty, what's your name?" he whispered as he removed his hand, stepping closer to my ear and rubbing his rock-hard dick against my ass to let me know how much he enjoyed the feel. I could tell he only asked my name to get close to me, but I told him anyway, even though it wasn't hard for him to find it out and he gave me his. The rest of the way to my cell, I explained to Officer Dontay Green that I was due to be released within the next week, and I would like to get to know him on a more personal level. He gave me his beautiful smile after locking me in my cell and whispered that he would make sure I had his number before I was released.

That night, I dreamed about Dontay. I dreamed some faceless bitch was trying to kill me and he was there to save me, only to give his own life for mine. I tried with all the power in me to fight, but I was no match for the automatic pistol she held. She tortured me, first shooting me in my left kneecap, forcing me to beg for my life.

I asked, "What have I done to deserve this?"

That's when she looked me in the eyes before stating, "Karma has arrived." With that being said, her face was now visible. It was

Shanel, looking back at me with an evil grin. The right side of her face was still missing as she turned slightly to the side to show me my work of art. I begged and apologized for my life, but the only results I got was Shanel reminding me that she got hers, so I needed to stop crying like a bitch and take mine like a big girl, before she fired her gun at my face.

I woke up breathing heavy and felt my face for any detachment, but only felt the dampness of my skin as everything was normal. I walked to the sink to wash my face and couldn't help but think about what that dream really meant. Could it mean Shanel was gone somehow come back for revenge? But how? I sat back down on my bed and thought about my mother, because she was always saying dreams were only God trying to warn you of something.

I walked to the door and looked out the window at the clock on the wall. It read twenty minutes past two in the am and I cursed myself, because I knew it would be a struggle for me to get back to sleep. Once I lay back down and tried, my mind quickly shifted to Dontay and how it would feel for him to make love to me. I slowly peeled off my jail uniform as my kitty became wet and I became greedy for the satisfying sensation. I began fingering myself and fondling my clit before picking up speed and wishing this was Dontay's dick, instead of my fingers working overtime on my kitty.

I lay all the way back, closed my eyes and my hands continued to work magic. I was so horny, my hips started to move against my hand on its own. My kitty longed for release as I finger-fucked myself and with the simple thought of Dontay, I was nearing my orgasm, which felt like it would quake the whole world.

"I'm almost there, Dontay, please make me cum," I moaned as I was close to approaching my state of satisfaction.

I continued invading my wetness, loving the sexual sounds it made and without warning, I let out a loud scream as I came, leaving a puddle on my bedsheets. I tried for round two, but tired and exhausted tears fell down my face, as I cried myself to sleep with my fingers still deep inside of my kitty.

Chapter 7

CoCo

Daniesse and I had begun to get kind of tight as the weeks passed. She confided a lot about her past to me and it really shocked me to the point that I felt sorry for her. She confirmed what I already figured the day I met her, and she admitted she was actually from St. Petersburg. One weekend on our girls' night out, she received a disturbing phone call, before advising me that she had to go to St. Pete for a family emergency. I forced her to let me go with her.

We arrived there faster than the ride normally was and then checked into the Ritz Carlton hotel right before night fell. While she went to take care of her family emergency, I walked across the street to rent me a car from Enterprise, because I had business of my own to take care of, fuck laying in a hotel room all day. I had a lot of shit on my mind and it was time to get it off, and since E'mani was still locked up, I felt like Mahogany was the next best thing.

Once I drove out the lot, I checked my magazine making sure I was ready for war, but I didn't really think it would come down to that, because once that bitch Mahogany was gone, E'mani wouldn't know what to do. I took some of the familiar roads and it wasn't long before I was pulling up in the driveway.

"Now or never, CoCo!" I said to hype myself up. I rechecked my magazine for what seemed like the hundredth time before exiting the car and walking towards the door. Every step I took, I felt like I was making the biggest mistake of my life, because Mahogany was like a sister to me.

All I could think about was the Baller Babies and the promise we made to always look out for each other but then again, I had to remind myself the Baller Babies was partly to blame for my twin sister not being here.

I knocked lightly on the door four times before I heard a familiar voice ask, "Who's there?" Without responding I knocked again, and the minute Mahogany snatched the door open, I fired three shots from my .380 right into her face, before I ran back to my car and drove away.

"I got her ass for you, Shanel, and if she make it up there to heaven with you, ask God for forgiveness after you beat that ass yourself," I shouted, feeling the adrenaline of putting in work. I rode by a sewage drain on my way back to the hotel and tossed the gun, after wiping it of my fingerprints. *I did what had to be done*, I thought as I couldn't stop my hands from shaking nervously. This wasn't my first body, so I didn't know why the hell I was feeling so damn shook. I really needed to get myself together.

Once I pulled into the parking garage of the Ritz Carlton, I shut off the engine, laid my seat all the way back and fired up a fat ass blunt of Loud. This was the only thing I knew to do that would calm me down and help me to think straight. I took big and long pulls, before holding the thick smoke until my lungs couldn't take the torture any longer and without coughing, I blew the smoke out with ease. I did this a couple more times, and the next thing I knew half an hour passed and I was still there, trying to convince myself I did the right thing.

I needed to get my ass up to the room, I'm pretty sure Daniesse was probably wondering where the hell I went. Ten minutes went by as I thought I was getting out of the car, but I was leaned over in between the driver seat and the car door. I tried again and this time, I actually made it out before making my way towards the hotel lobby.

People greeted me and some of them even took the courtesy of holding the door open, but my face stayed scrunched up as if I just ate a lemon, ignoring their act of kindness. The elevator ride felt like it took a whole hour to get to my floor and I was damn near sleep, until the loud bell woke me up indicating that I had reached my floor. I struggled to retrieve my key card out of my purse and just as I was about to unlock the door it flew open, causing me to damn near fall through the threshold.

"Long night, huh?" Daniesse asked as we both looked at the digital clock on the nightstand beside the bed. I ignored her walking straight to the bed not realizing that the murder was already all over the news. All I wanted to do was sleep and that's exactly what I did soon as my head touched the pillow.

When I woke up about eight hours later, Daniesse was nowhere to be found. I brushed it off as she was probably still handling whatever business she had with her family. I ordered room service before getting in the shower as my head throbbed and I could feel a hangover easing in.

These damn drugs were starting to take a toll on me, because not only was I a heavy smoker of Loud and Molly, but I had recently started lacing my blunts with Percocets and occasionally Xanax to get me where I wanted to be. That was something I kept though, because I could never forget the way Mahogany, Nah Nah, Nicole and E'mani acted the day I let all them bitches smoke my shit, and when I told them I laced Molly with the Loud, them bitches wanted to beat my ass.

I also didn't need people judging me or trying to serve me in front of the whole world. I laughed at myself before shaking my head as the shower water rained on my body. I really couldn't believe the turn my life took and I couldn't blame my sister's death, because my habit started long before she was killed. I needed a change, but until Mahogany and E'mani both were dead, I needed every blunt I could handle to keep me level-headed.

A minute or two later, I heard a knock on the front door and proceeded to get out the shower. I wrapped a towel around my body, but almost ran back in the bathroom when the cool breeze tackled me. I didn't know why the hell Daniesse had the damn A.C. up so fuckin high, but my dumb ass walked right past the thermostat to answer the door and didn't adjust it. I knew it was most likely room service, but I still asked who was there. No one answered, so I peeped out the peephole before opening it. Surprised that nobody was there, I still looked up and down the hallway, before picking up the package that lay at my feet then closed the door back.

What the hell is this? I thought as I shook it, before placing it to my ear for any type of sound. The box was wrapped in blood red paper with a bow on top of it. I knew it wasn't a bomb, because I didn't hear it ticking or maybe I had a secret admirer. I smiled excitedly. I unwrapped the box, thinking of the last person I shared a sample of this good pussy with, but quickly got confused when I saw the ugliest black dress I have ever seen.

I pulled it up to my body before checking myself in the mirror and agreed it wasn't my style. *Who the hell was this thing from?* I wondered until I saw a card with my name on it that read, "You couldn't hide from us, we know who you are, we know where you are and the timer on your life is running out. We could've bodied your ass already, but we wanted to have a little fun so in the meantime, here's a black dress you could wear to your funeral, so your family wouldn't have to buy one. Just think of it as a favor from me to you because we know it was you, so you might want to go ahead and kill yourself before we do."

I snapped back from the sudden daydream to find myself still in the shower. Damn, I was really losing my mind and at that moment, I was starting to second guess my actions as if I was afraid of the Baller Babies. The whole world knew if they wanted me dead, they would be coming with their guns blazing and besides, I already put three bullets in Mahogany's face yesterday, so I know them two new bitches didn't want no smoke.

I wonder if it was God, trying to send me a message or something. I know I've done some fucked-up shit to people and I know I can't expect karma not to come for me, but why me? Why do I have to be the one karma wants? I've asked God for forgiveness on many occasions. Then I thought about all the people I've killed, all the people I've hurt, all the ones that begged for their lives and I didn't care, all because the Baller Babies were trying to make a name for ourselves.

I jumped from the sudden noise of somebody knocking on the door again. I didn't know what to think after that daydream because everything was starting to feel like déjà vu. "Should I answer it?" I asked myself but jumped out the shower anyway, before wrapping a towel around myself. I fumbled around the room, looking for anything I could use for protection in case they came in, but cried when I couldn't.

Tears fell down my face, because I knew it was my time, and the only thing I could do was take it like I gave it. I sat on the floor with my back against the bed and my knees to my chest when I heard the doorknob turn as if somebody were trying to enter. I asked God for forgiveness one last time but when I looked up, the door opened with Daniesse walking through it.

"Girl, what the hell is you doing in here laying on the floor half-naked? You got the damn shower water running, fogging the whole fuckin room up, and then you got room service out here waiting on your ass. What the fuck is wrong with you?" she said with much attitude. I could see her grab the food from room service before tipping him and sending him on his way. I slowly stood to my feet, wondering should I tell her what's been going on since my day started. I mean, she needed to know, if the shit came true and they actually came to the room and hurt us.

"Daniesse, I think some—"

"I don't want to hear it, CoCo, you out here going crazy on them fuckin drugs. Yeah, I know all about the pills you lace your weed with. You left all your residue on the fuckin table last night," she snapped, cutting me off before I even got the whole sentence out of my mouth.

I stared at her with an attitude, but the second she locked eyes with me I dropped my head from embarrassment. It killed me inside that she knew about my habit. I felt so dirty and unwanted, I couldn't move fast enough as I grabbed my clothes and locked myself in the bathroom. I jumped back in the shower and stood under the showerhead as the water rained on me for the second time in thirty minutes. The water was steaming and before I knew it, I was lathering my rag with soap and scrubbing my skin raw.

I was trying to scrub away the years of secrets I promised myself I would take to my grave, all the years I used drugs as a way of coping with the secrets I held in, and the memories of my sister with half of her fuckin face blown off. I was holding so much in, I felt like I could explode at any second if I didn't find a way to let it all out.

Twenty minutes passed before I decided to get out the shower, then proceeded to dry myself off. I knew what I needed to do to get my mind right and that's all I thought about as I made my way out the bathroom, before getting dressed and heading to my car. I drove around for thirty whole minutes, trying to get my thoughts together and before I knew it, I was entering the cemetery where Shanel, Nah Nah and Nicole had been buried.

This was the first time I've been here since their funerals and the closer I was to her grave, the more I realized I really needed to talk to my sister. I tried to keep my emotions in check, because Shanel wouldn't have that crying shit, but I couldn't help it as I stared at her tombstone. Why it had to be her and not me? I mean, she was the good twin, she didn't deserve what she got.

I started to think about what our mother always told us when we were younger. Karma is real, and it will come when you least expect it. It doesn't have to come after you just because you're the one who did wrong. It may get somebody you love like your sister, brother, mother, father or even your kids and grandkids but it will always come because you reap what you sow. I felt like I was the reason my sister wasn't living today, because I can't begin to explain all the wrong I've done, but this was my chance to confess and apologize to her for all the hurt I caused her.

"Top of the morning, Shanel, I know I haven't been here to visit and right now I don't have an excuse, so all I can say is I'm sorry. I just been going through so much since you been gone, and I feel like my karma is the reason you're not with me anymore." I stopped to wipe my eyes, not wanting to cry as I dropped to my knees in front of her tombstone. "Well, I'm not going to beat around the bush, because I think you deserve to know, so here goes my confession. Do you remember the night your boyfriend Trey got killed? I was the girl the news said was with him when the police showed up. I just gave an alias name.

"Trey and I was having sex behind your back for over two years and I started to get emotionally attached to him. I thought I was very much in love, so I told him he needed to break up with you, so him and I could run to Vegas and get married. Well, he laughed in my face and told me this was our last time together before threatening to tell you everything if I didn't call it quits. I didn't want it to be over because he was the only man that made me feel special and complete whenever we were together.

"So, after weeks of trying to make him love me and failing, I came up with an idea. That night, I tricked him to the motel room I had by informing him that you were hurt and needed him. Once he arrived, he was a little pissed when he didn't see you, but I convinced him to stay and promised this would be our last night together. We had sex over and over again for four whole hours, until we both were tired and exhausted.

"When he got up to use the bathroom, I made a phone call I've regretted every day since that night, because it killed you along with him. Thirty minutes later, two masked men kicked the door open, shot Trey in the head and then tore the room up to make it look like a robbery gone bad. I felt like if he didn't want me and I couldn't have him, then nobody would have him."

To my surprise, I didn't feel the urge to cry as I continued to stare at Shanel's picture engraved in her headstone. I really did feel bad for what I did, but at the same time, it felt good to finally get it out of my system. I looked around, noticing I was still alone but felt embarrassed anyway, because I knew Nah Nah and Nicole were listening to every word I was saying as well.

I wanted to get up and leave right then, but something told me to stay and let everything out to free myself of the demons I was fighting. "I'm so sorry, Shanel, if I could turn back time I would," I started back as I stared at her picture again. "That's not all though, and I know you might never forgive me for this, but I have to tell you. I had a feeling Mahogany and E'mani had something to do with your death, so without question, I wanted revenge. No, I don't have solid evidence and I really don't know if it's true, but I went to the house and shot Mahogany three times in the face, killing her.

"E'mani is in jail and if she beats her charge, I will get her to and won't lose any sleep behind it. I'm just sorry for you because I know you wouldn't want that to happen, but I don't see it that way.

Rest in peace, Shanel, I love you." That was the last thing I said before walking away.

Chapter 8

Mahogany

"Oh my God, yes, eat me like it's your last meal," I moaned, feeling the urge to cum building up. Rue was driving me crazy with his tongue and the way he was satisfying me, I must say I couldn't complain.

We had only been seeing each other for a little while and I can't lie, it felt like love at first sight for the both of us, at least that's what he told me. And I'm ashamed to say I gave the pussy up after only knowing him for a week, so fuck what Steve Harvey was saying in his book titled, *Act Like a Lady, Think Like a Man*. He claimed the only way a bitch would really know if her man would take her serious or love her when they first meet is to make him wait three months to get the pussy.

First of all, that's a damn lie. If a man love you, he love you no matter if you gave up the pussy on the first day or waited a whole year to give it to him. Second, why the hell would I wait three months? Don't all the stupid bitches who bought his book know they are depriving themselves of some good dick and possibly a golden head?

I made him stop for a minute while I got up from the position I was in, and turned around so I was on my hands and knees with my fat ass in the air, before giving him the green light to continue eating the pussy like he got it fifty percent off with a coupon.

"Shit, yeah! Lick my clit in circles, baby, spell your name on that muthafucka. Let me know this pussy belongs to Rue," I moaned out of control, while encouraging him and expecting the neighbors to show up any minute now, thinking somebody was getting killed. Well, actually somebody was doing some killing and if it could happen, my little pussy would've had a toe tag right about now.

While I was enjoying orgasm after orgasm, without warning, Rue slid his fingers in my pussy before stroking them down over my clit and then back up towards my ass. I was so wet it felt as if somebody poured a whole bottle of water over my midsection, so his tongue and fingers were slipping and sliding, while bringing me orgasms that made me tap out from sensitivity and exhaustion. Now, I usually don't suck dick, and let me be the first to say I'm far from a golden head, but something made me want to try it with Rue.

He lay on his back with his hands behind his head as I slowly started stroking his dick. It felt so soft against my hand, but hard as a rock at the same time as I stared at the mushroom-like head. I really couldn't believe I was about to do it, but my heart wanted me to show him the same pleasure he showed me. I took a deep breath after witnessing Rue laugh at me for my lack of experience and went for the gusto. My open mouth lingered just inches from his manhood and my intentions really were to go all the way, but the sound of three gunshots caused the both of us to scramble for our weapons before aiming them at each other.

"Bitch, you tryna set me up? Ha, I knew you were just too good to be true. Damn! How the fuck I let you get me like this?" Rue spit, thinking I was playing some type of game with his life. He really had me feeling some type of way, because while he was over there trying to play mind games like I was the one tryna set him up, he knew just as well it was the other way around. Bitches and even niggas knew not to show up to Mahogany's house wanting smoke, because they knew the results, so that had to be Rue's people downstairs.

"Listen, baby." I started laughing to defuse the situation because we weren't getting anywhere standing here with guns pointed at each other. "I'm not tryna set you up, you gotta believe me. Now, whoever is down there will probably make their way up here if we both don't go check it out." He stared at me, with his gun still aimed at my head. I tried to give him my most sensitive look to prove I was telling the truth and I guess it worked because he started slowly lowering his gun.

We both threw on a pair of boxer shorts and a t-shirt before making our way downstairs. I followed his lead with my gun aimed and ready to shoot anything that moved. I was hoping for the best, while at the same time preparing for the worse, because I didn't know what to expect when we made it to the first floor of the house. "Don't let it be, God please don't let it be," Rue shouted the second we saw the body of a woman laid out on the floor in a puddle of blood.

I was confused because it seemed as if Rue knew this woman, but what I wanted to know was, what the hell she doing in my house? Rue dropped to his knees to check her neck for a pulse and I could tell he knew she was dead the minute he turned her head towards us, you could never mistake the cold, spaced-out look of death. He stood up, now facing me and noticing the look on my face, I guess he felt the need to explain.

"That's my little sister. I brought with me to watch my back because I don't trust too many people. I didn't know if I was getting set up or not, but I told her to stay in the car. Damn, why didn't she listen to me!" he shouted as he hit the wall with a closed fist.

I stepped into his space and gave him a hug, doing my best to comfort him. I wasn't very good at this kind of stuff but again, I was willing to try for Rue. *Who could have disrespected my house*, was all I thought about as I enjoyed the feel of Rue in my arms, but then I ignored the thought for the time being, wanting to give him my full attention. He gave me a look without saying a word, and I knew I had to do my part by calling 911 and reporting the death while he disappeared. Hell, I didn't want all them muthafuckin pigs in my house, but I checked my attitude, answered their questions and did what I had to do until I was able to get away and talk to Rue.

"Baby, everything good on my end. They just left about ten minutes ago. I'm cleaning up the house now," I spoke once I heard Rue's voice. It was three o'clock in the damn morning and I was so tired from dealing with them damn pigs all night, but tired or not I still wanted Rue here with me when I decided to watch the security footage of what really happened. Honestly, I was surprised they didn't notice the camera sitting outside my front door, the way that bitch stood out like a sore thumb, but knowing them sorry mutha-fuckas, their only mission was trying to find a black person to blame all this shit on. I told Rue about the footage and what my plans were before hanging up.

He sounded just as eager as I was when he stated, "I'm on my way, don't do anything until I get there."

I held my composure much as I could, but really felt like a muthafucka disrespected my house by pulling some shit like this. I could tell there wasn't any sign of forced entry and that meant the door was either unlocked, or Rue's sister opened it to let the shooter in. But why the fuck would she open the damn door for somebody she didn't know? And not only that, I still don't know if the shooter came looking for me or followed Rue's ass here. I kept going over different scenarios but couldn't seem to come up with one that was closer to the truth of what happened. I just didn't know anybody who would have the balls to show up to my house and let their guns bust.

Rue finally showed up after thirty minutes and wrapped his arms around my body, slightly scaring me but damn, *it feels good to be in his arms*, I thought before I turned around to put my lips on his. We both knew I was falling for him and I loved the feeling, but then again, I didn't like how soft I was becoming. I didn't even let my guard down this much with Supreme. Now that I think about it, I was really about to put my mouth on Rue's dick and give him head. Supreme never got that from me and his bitch ass knew not to even ask.

"Where's the video, baby?" Rue asked breaking me out of my daydream. I grabbed his hand and led him back to my room without further verbal communication. I wanted to know what really happened as much as he did, but something in me had to know if he was always on point as much as he thought he was.

"Baby, I remember you telling me you still had smoke with a couple niggas from your past, but tell me this, do you know if you could've been followed here and not realized it?" I said as I stared in his eyes. waiting on an honest answer. He frowned up his face before turning his head to look me deep in my eyes as he softly bit down on his bottom lip.

"Honestly?" he started, turning his head back towards the TV screen like he was watching something. "I can't even tell you because I don't know. I was so eager to finally spend some time with you that it never crossed my mind I could've been followed."

Just as I thought, he was your typical nigga, always lettin pussy take priority over what was really important. His own damn life or in this case, his sister's. I hated to see a man let that emotion became his weakness because if a bitch wanted to rob or even kill him, all she had to do was let him smell the sweet aroma of her pussy and guess what? She got his ass hypnotized. No bullshit, I really wanted this relationship to work, so it was important that I drop some jewels on him. Even if he didn't listen, he'll always remember what I said.

"Baby, if we gone be a team, I feel it's my position as your queen to let my king know what's in the best interest of the both of us. Now, I know men gone be men and fuck around, they could have the most flawless bitch in the world at home and would still creep around. I don't understand that, but hey, who am I to try and understand something that's not meant to be understood? My only concern is that you come back to me, and don't let yourself become a victim of a robbery or murder, just because you see a bitch with a fat ass and a wet pussy. You catching my drift?" I asked, not really wanting him to say anything, but at the same time letting me know he was paying attention. He shook his head as if he understood, but really didn't convince me as much as he thought.

"Naw bae, you not hearing what I'm saying. I'm talking about any bitch, even me. Example, earlier when you were on your way over here, you were thinking about my pussy and how good you would fuck me. Which clouded your mind and distracted you from being on point and watching your surroundings to see if you were being followed, shit like that is what I'm talking about."

Now I could tell I had his attention and he's thinking about everything I just said, because he knew I was right. Mahogany is a real bitch and I know how real bitches think, so everything I spit is facts. I don't talk just because I have lips.

With that being said, I left him to his thoughts as I moved towards the TV to set up everything so we could watch the security footage. The TV showed a blue screen for the first two minutes and then the front of my house popped up. The next couple minutes, all we saw was birds flying before we started to get impatient but as I was getting up to switch the scene, we saw a baby blue Chevy Malibu pull into the driveway.

"Hold up, baby," Rue said, stopping me before I could touch anything. I slowly sat back down without taking my eyes off the screen as a woman stepped out the car. I looked closer, trying to make out the identity of the mystery woman as she began walking towards my front door. For the life of me, I couldn't figure out who this bitch was, until she reached the first step of my porch and looked directly into the camera without knowing it.

"Oh, my fuckin God!" I spoke out loud without knowing it. *It was CoCo who killed Rue's sister,* I thought as I continued to watch as she knocked on the door. Once it was opened, she let off three shots and was halfway to her car by the time Rue's sister hit the floor.

"Oh, my fuckin God!" I caught myself saying again. I just couldn't believe CoCo would do some shit like this. We were supposed to be family, Double B's for life, and this bitch disrespected my shit like that? I felt so fuckin dumb right now because here I was, thinking all this was Rue's fault for not being on point and letting somebody follow him to my house, and it was my sister that killed his sister.

"I take it you know who this lady is that killed my sister?" Rue asked after witnessing the expression that was left on my face from being caught by surprise. I couldn't say anything as I looked at him with an expressionless look on my face. My words caught in my throat and I couldn't speak if I wanted to, which I didn't. How could I tell the man I'm in love with, that the woman I loved like a sister was the one responsible for his sister's death?

"I'm guessing I'm talking to my damn self, since my girl—"

"What you want me to say, Rue?" I snapped, cutting him off before he could finish his sentence. "The bitch I considered family and loved like a sister, disrespected my house and shot the sister of the man I love. Now I have to risk losing you over something I had nothing to do with." I started crying because I was under a lot of pressure and I really didn't know what to do.

He sat there and stared at me. I mean, he didn't even try to hide the fact that he was trying to look to my soul to find out if I was lying or not. We were both quiet now, but Rue silence was killing me more, because I had no idea of knowing what the hell was on his mind.

"Honestly, bae, it's a lot of bullshit going through my mind right now and I don't know what to believe. But you telling me that you had nothing to do with the death of my sister?" he finally spoke, even though he was basically telling me he didn't believe what I was saying. I nervously shook my head yes and started to plead my case a little more but was stopped by his deep demanding voice.

"Prove it! Prove to me that you love me and that you had nothing to do with my sister getting killed. You say the bitch you treated like a sister disrespected your house, so that means she disrespected you. Now show me what you do to bitches that disrespects you."

I wiped away my tears and tried to show him I wasn't a weak bitch, but it wasn't hard to decipher what Rue was saying. He wanted me to end CoCo's life. And to prove my love and loyalty to him, Coco was a dead bitch walking, believe that.

Keith Williams

Chapter 9

E'mani

Twelve o'clock struck and like Cinderella, I was rushing to get home. Michael Conn kept his word and got me out of this hell hole that locked me down twenty-three hours a damn day, and I was so fuckin thankful. To my surprise, Dontay escorted me to the front to be dressed out. I couldn't complain enough about how embarrassed I was to put back on the same stale smelling ass outfit I got arrested in almost four months ago.

He acted as if he didn't notice the smell when he gave me a hug and slipped his cell number into my pocket, but I knew I stunk, and it didn't sit too well with me. He left within a couple of minutes thought to get back to work and I was stuck in a daydream like a young schoolgirl fantasizing about him again.

"E'mani!" I heard somebody yell and by the way they said it, I could tell it wasn't the first time. I turned towards the voice with my set up ready to illustrate and beat a bitch ass, thinking I had finally caught Officer Davis by herself.

"Hold up Laila Ali, it's just me. I don't want no smoke," Mahogany joked, surprising the hell out of me at the same time. We both embraced in a bear hug as if it had been years since we last saw each other. I couldn't believe I was finally free, and it felt damn good to feel the love from my sister, as she showed me that she missed me as much as I missed her.

"Damn girl, you smelling kind of stale. I hope you were washing your ass in there, because you know we don't play that shit," she joked, putting her hands on my chest to put space between us. I can't lie, hearing that shit from Mahogany, joke or not, really made me feel more embarrassed and I kind of wanted to cry. But one positive thing jail did do for me was made me tough, and I couldn't let myself show no weak emotions.

"This whole fuckin jail smell stale and if you would've brought me some more clothes to wear, I wouldn't be rocking the same darn shit I got arrested in four months ago and you wouldn't have to smell my ass," I shot back. We both burst into laughter before hugging again and then turned our backs to Pinellas County Jail. We drove straight home, which I requested because I couldn't and wouldn't dare let anybody else see me like this.

A bitch had pride, even when I just got out the county jail on protective custody. Well, just to set the record straight, how many people really think a muthafucka would believe E'mani Newman, a member of one of the most dangerous crews in Florida did her county bid on P.C.? Nobody and besides, I'll just lie or have the bitch spraying me killed, simple as that.

Once we pulled up to the house, I got out the car as Mahogany remained seated. She explained she had business to take care of and would be back in an hour or so. I didn't really think too much of it. My main focus was throwing away these stank ass clothes before soaking in some hot water. I walked into the house and looked around as if it was my first time ever being here. There was something different about the place, I just couldn't put my finger on it.

I continued my tour making my way upstairs and into my room. Everything there looked the same, actually it doesn't look like anybody even been in here, but I did a quick inspection anyway. Once I was satisfied, I grabbed my tablet and played my favorite playlist so I could relax to Alicia Keys' soothing voice. That girl could sing her ass off. A lot of people like Whitney Houston and I can't take anything from her, because the whole world knew she could definitely blow, but Alicia Keys is more of my era, not Whitney.

I grabbed my strawberry scented bath and body wash, my panties and bra and then made my way to the bathroom. Once naked, I stared at my body in the mirror behind the door and couldn't believe it. Minus the fact that I need to shave, it was evident I gained weight and anybody that knew me would admit it, but what amazed me was that it was all in the right places. My ass became rounder, my hips grew wider and my D-cup breasts were so perky that an eighteen-year-old teenager had nothing on me.

I couldn't really say what my measurements were, but if I had to guess, I would say 34-25-45. Yeah, a real certified bad bitch. I was feeling myself so much right now, I felt I could challenge Mahogany in a twerk battle and win. She was good at it, because she grew up dancing, but I had confidence in myself.

I changed the song on my tablet from Alicia Keys to Trap Beckham's "Hit It," and started making my ass jump like a jack rabbit with ADHD. I twerked all the way to the floor before going into a split, then mimicked myself riding a dick while bouncing one cheek and then both cheeks. Once I was back on my feet again, I rested my right leg on the sink and continued twerking in the mirror as I made the dancers in Nicki Minaj's music video, "Anaconda," look like amateurs.

Hot and sweaty, the song went off and I ran myself a bath while I shaved my legs, my kitty and my armpits before relaxing in the warm, strawberry-scented water. Anybody who's a fan of part one should already know that once I'm in the tub, twenty minutes could easily turn into thirty, thirty into forty then the next thing I know, a whole hour went by. Well, today is no different and I was feeling so relaxed that I dozed off and didn't awake until I felt the temperature of the water changed.

"E'mani! Girl, get your ass out the damn shower, you're not in jail no more. Water isn't free," Mahogany yelled as she banged on the bathroom door before laughing. I smirked and turned my nose up towards the door, even though she couldn't see me. I guess some things never change about people. Here she was taking my incarceration as a joke, when honestly, I didn't see a damn thing funny about me fighting for my life.

"I'm just teasing you girl, but fa'real, I got some people I want you to meet." I stood up in the tub, drained the water out and then turned on the shower to rinse myself before getting out. I can't lie, I really enjoyed that bath. Sometimes, people forget and take for granted the simple things in life until it's taken away. Before I went to jail, I never in a million years appreciated taking a bath so much.

I dried off, then threw on my black and red panty and bra set before exiting the bathroom and entering my bedroom. I took my time lotioning my body before throwing on a pantsuit by Ms. Cat. Satisfied with my outfit, I quickly curled my hair, then threw on some lip gloss and before I knew it, I was on my way downstairs with the confidence of a bitch whose shit didn't stank.

I had a chance to see everybody before they noticed I was there and that gave me the opportunity to analyze their characters, so I stared like they all were from foreign counties. Mahogany was doing the talking and from the way she was demonstrating, I could tell nothing about her had changed. She was the same bitch that would give up her own life for the only family she had, the Baller Babies!

The other two females I didn't know, and really didn't care to know if they weren't screaming Double B's. They seemed to be paying close attention to every word that fell out of Mahogany's mouth. I don't know if that was a good or bad thing, but I just prayed they had minds of their own and didn't let the fame of the Baller Babies define who they are.

The man, on the other hand, looked good enough to eat, I mean literally. His waves were on point, his swag was screaming "join the wave" and he smelled like money was the brand of the expensive cologne he had on. He reminded me a lot of Supreme, not from the way he looked, but from the way he gave off the energy that he was the boss man.

Mahogany was still speaking and in return, I stood there as if I thought they were speaking about me. I really wasn't too good at this eavesdropping thing because I couldn't hear shit, so without another thought, I stepped into the living room making my presence known. Everybody became quiet before looking around at each other and it tickled me on the inside, because I knew they were wondering if I heard anything I wasn't supposed to hear.

"It's about time you made it down here. I was starting to think you were sleep and having dreams about Supreme fucking you to death again," Mahogany joked, trying to break the awkward silence. I quickly shot her daggers because she knew she was dead wrong for going there and offering my business to everybody. "You know I'm just joking, girl. But everybody, meet the infamous E'mani. Yeah, the one we just put all that work in for."

I smiled so everybody wouldn't feel uncomfortable and think I was a stuck-up bitch who couldn't take a joke. Honestly, I really did appreciate everything they did for me because jail is not for me, I probably would've done a Shanel and tried to hang myself if they would've found me guilty of that murder. I'll never let anybody know that though because that suicide shit make you look to weak. She continued the introductions and I found out the man's name was Rue. He was Mahogany's man. The little brother of a brick mason and he was what you would call a made man. He kinda put you in the mind of Moneybag Yo, with his brown-paper-bag skin complexion and tattoos in his face, but I'll just keep that comment to myself.

Next, she introduced the two girls standing closer to me as Champagne and Passion. Now I wasn't no lesbian, but I can appreciate the sight of beautiful women when I see them. She went on to explain these were the two bitches who had been keeping the Baller Babies' name alive and were on the verge of having more bodies under their belts than Shoot'em Up.

I can't lie, that impressed me because I low-key looked up to Shoot'em Up and was tryna get my body count up there with hers, until the reality that I'm not untouchable caught up to me. I shook their hands and gave all three of them a hug as if saying welcome to the team before Mahogany mentioned that we were on a tight schedule and that it was time to go.

Upon entering the double doors that led into Club Paid, Mahogany, Champagne, Passion and I became the center of attention with all eyes on us as we strutted across the marbled floor, looking like supermodels. Mahogany sported a white Chanel dress, with a thigh-high split down the side and her back completely out. White and silver Chanel pumps graced her freshly pedicured feet and her hair fell down her back in loose curls, with a part down the middle.

Champagne and Passion, on the other hand, both sashayed in Donna Karan skinny jeans, which fit like gloves on their figures, a white and pink fitted tee for Champagne and a gold one for Passion. Donna Karan pumps decorated their feet and they wore their hair pinned into an updo, complementing their features.

I continued to rock my pantsuit by Ms. Cat and was positive I was the reason for all the attention we were receiving. We found a table up against the wall all the way in the back, but the minute DJ Red Eye spotted us, he shouted out the Baller Babies like we were the guests of honor. I smiled and waved, but automatically noticed all the surprise expressions some people gave as they could finally put faces with the bitches' names that had the whole state of Florida shook.

He then sent a special shout out to me, welcoming me home with bottles of Cîroc. I can't lie, at the moment all the fake love made me feel good as a dozen women and men I had never met a day in my life, screamed welcome as if we've been friends since day one. One by one, me and my girls took shots to celebrate my freedom and death to our future haters. I wanted to get "white girl wasted" tonight, because I felt being sober would only bring back the memories of my last couple months behind bars.

After about ten minutes and five shots, I grabbed my girls and pulled them to the dance floor as our anthem, "Diva," by Beyoncé flowed through the speakers. "A diva is a female version of a hustla!" we all sang as we swung our hips and seductively ran our hands all over our bodies.

It wasn't long before niggas started to get in our space like straight groupies and of course, we politely chucked up the deuces to each one of them and continued having a good time. We knew what time it was, they all were either tryna get fame off our name, by acting like they knew us the way people did Big Meech and BMF, or tryna put their bid in for a taste of this rare breed, Baller Baby pussy. I can't tell you which one, but they were really starting to fuck up a bitch's vibe. I was riding and really starting to feel the effect of the liquor as I went to the table to grab a whole bottle.

"Double B's, bitches!" I heard Mahogany yell, followed by Champagne and then Passion, as they popped bottle after bottle of liquor before spraying each other.

It felt good to be free and as everybody told me, "Welcome Home" for the hundredth time, I turned up with my girls by jumping on the stage and twerking like I practiced in the bathroom earlier. I don't know if it was the liquor in my system or if I just wanted to do it, but I found myself locking lips with a random girl and I was enjoying it, until I thought about Kayla. I can't say I was gone start bumping pussy, because I was strickly-dickly, and you could never replace the feel of a man, for a woman. But her soft lips felt good against mine, because it's been a while since I've had that body part of a person so close to mine, man or woman.

We all knew about the situation the Baller Babies went through with Kayla and her lover, and I wasn't trying to give anybody the impression that I was bicurious, so I stepped back to apologize. The minute we looked into each other's eyes, all I could see was terror as she tried to speak, but no words could be heard over the loud voice of Post Malone and my girls screaming, "Double B's!" I turned around to get an understanding of what had her so shocked and all I saw was darkness, after feeling two powerful blows to my stomach.

Keith Williams

Chapter 10

CoCo

This year had really been a hell of a year for me. It's like, first I was on top of the world, and had all I wanted in the palm of my hand, once the Baller Babies got back together after five long years. But then, a black cloud flew over us and murder was all I saw. First Nah Nah, followed by Nicole, then Shanel and last, Mahogany. Death was like a frequent episode in my life and I felt the walls were closing in on me, which meant I would be next. Honestly, I was willing to take what was coming for me, because Lord knows I wasn't a saint, but first I had to get revenge for my sister by ending E'mani's life.

That night, I confessed my involvement and dislike for the Baller Babies to Daniesse. I told her how it all started, from our time locked up together to Supreme getting killed, E'mani getting arrested and why I killed Mahogany. At the same time wanting E'mani dead. I told her everything, which kept us up until the wee hours of the morning and at the same time helped me to relieve some of the stress I was feeling, because she was a damn good listener and gave me feedback when it was needed.

I could tell she was surprised from the expression left on her face, but what she confessed to me outweighed the little shocker I gave her. Everything made sense though and I now understood why she dropped everything to come to St. Pete and why she's always gone when I wake up. I would've never in a million years thought fate would bring the two of us together.

Once we did call it a night, I thought hard about what Daniesse told me and felt like things were really about to get complicated before I drifted off to sleep. It was around twelve pm when the sun's rays forced me to wake up and like any other day, I found myself alone because Daniesse was gone in the wind. I thought about calling her to see if she wanted to do lunch but changed my mind, just before I dialed her number.

I wanted to have some fun today. I was tired of being in this damn room, where all I did was stare at four walls as if I was in a prison cell. Daniesse left me her personal Glock 9 to protect myself and I still had contact with some of my girls in the city who knew where the ballers would be. So, just like the old days, it was time for the city to know CoCo was back in this bitch.

Dressed in my Christian Dior pantsuit and red bottom pumps, I was looking like a movie star as I drove my rented baby blue Malibu all the way to the other side of town to hang out with my girl, Tay. It had been a while since the two of us had a chance to kick it and I was really looking forward to it.

"C'mon, girl! I'm ready to get fucked up and turn up like the old days," I said, before blowing my horn to let Tay know I was outside. We were supposed to meet her old man and his friend at the club. You know, something like a double date.

Standing only five foot two, with dark skin and a petite frame, Tay looked like a model for real in her Ralph Lauren halter top and mini skirt. We hugged before kissing each other on the cheek as she got into the car.

"Girl, you don't know how much I miss you right now. It's been forever since the last time we kicked it," Tay said, while putting on her seat belt. I sat there and stared, noticing how she'd picked up weight around her hips and thighs since I'd last seen her. I didn't want to say anything, because I didn't know if she was insecure about it or not, but I definitely noticed. When she finally got herself together, I guess she felt me watching her, because she looked right into my eyes.

"Why are you looking at me like a starstruck fan?" she wanted to know. I caught myself after hearing her voice and had no choice but to confess that I was admiring how thick she had gotten. I guess she took it as a compliment, because she started smiling like somebody who just got new teeth.

"You can thank Moe for that. All that man wanna do is beat the pussy up like it was a dolla short on a payment." I covered my mouth to prevent spit from flying everywhere and laughed before putting the car in drive and taking off.

It wasn't long before we made it to the club, and the line was all the way around the building. I mean literally. People were about to start a fight over being skipped. I found a parking spot before we walked back to the front and damn near changed my mind when I thought we had to get at the end of the line.

"Swift owns the club, so everything is on him tonight. I wish I would have to stand in line like these broke ass hoes. I'd never come to the club," Tay said, while pulling out her cell to call her man and let him know we were outside waiting. Not even two minutes after she hung up, the bouncer at the door removed the velvet rope to let us in, VIP style. We both sashayed like the bad bitches we were and laughed as we heard the hating ass comments the bitches in line made about us.

Once we did make it inside, we were met by a woman who introduced herself, before escorting us to the table where two gentlemen were sitting. I could see four women on the other side of the club turnt up and riding the wave of the music, but it was too dark to recognize them, so I stood there in my Tyra Banks pose as Tay introduced everybody. "Baby, this is my friend CoCo I was telling you about. CoCo, this is my boyfriend Moe and his friend, Swift."

We all shook hands and gave each other friendly smiles before sitting down. I sat beside Swift after enjoying the sight of his dark chocolate skin, five-ten frame and head full of waves. I still couldn't get past the fact that my girl snatched up a good-looking man herself. Moe stood about the same height as Swift, and cocoa-butter skin with a clean-cut bald head, reminding me of the actor Common.

"What you ladies drinking tonight?" Swift asked, breaking me out of my daydream.

Tay and I both looked at each other and at the same time shouted, "Rozay," mimicking Rick Ross, before bursting into laughter. Swift smiled at us but went to the bar and came back with two bottles. The bottles were almost empty by the time everybody started to loosen up and I was ready to grab Tay and hit the dance floor until "Slow Motion" by Trey Songz played through the speakers and Swift asked me to dance.

Keith Williams

I looked at Tay as if I was getting her approval before I said, "Yes," then put my hand in his while he led the way. I wrapped my arms around his neck, and he slid his hands around my waist before palming my ass, I guess to feel how soft it was. I looked him in the eyes and smiled to let him know a bitch didn't mind giving up the pussy, but it wasn't gone be cheap. We danced through four songs and didn't have any plans of slowing down.

Tay and Moe sat at the table playing kissy-face all night while stealing glances at Swift and me to make sure we were getting along. I watched them the whole time they watched us and by the way she was grinding on his lap, I could tell she was getting horny. It wasn't long before her nasty ass grabbed Moe's hand and hid it under her skirt like they were playing hide the hand, and the minute he reached home base his eyes bulged, letting me know she wasn't wearing panties. I kept watching as she closed her eyes and threw her head back, enjoying the pleasure Moe was giving her. She started grinding again, this time a little harder and even though it was dark in here, I still caught her "O" face.

I was starting to feel Swift's dick pressing up against my ass as we danced and I can't front, that nigga was turning me on. I knew sooner than later, he too would be ready to explode if I kept throwing it back on him like I was, so I smiled at him before suggesting we take a break. I led the way this time by walking in front of him to hide his hard-on as we headed back to our table.

The second we approached, I spotted Tay sitting on Moe's lap with her skirt hiked a little, and the inside of her thighs were white as if she had powdered them before we arrived. She looked up to see my eyes and quickly lifted herself to pull her skirt down, but as she did so, I caught an eye full of Moe's erect dick bulging through his shorts. Swift was still standing behind me tryna hide his own erection, so his attention was somewhere else. But, like a bitch in the comfort of her own home, Tay simply got off Moe's dick and proceeded towards the ladies' room, with me right behind her. I noticed it was empty as I checked every stall for a pair of feet before locking the door. We stood face-to-face in front of the mirror, waiting for the other to break the silence.

78

"Girl, what the fuck is wrong with you? You got to be crazy to let that nigga fuck you in a damn club where any fuckin body could see. Do you know how much of a hoe that make you look like?" I shouted, clearly upset about how my friend was so open when it came to sex. She looked at me with a stale face and I knew she was wondering how I, her friend, could stand here and judge her.

"I can't believe out of all people... you're standing here judging me. Bitch please, don't you forget I was there when you were deep throating Shanel's boyfriend's dick, while she was asleep on the same bed right next to y'all, or how you fucked your mother's man and then lied about him cheating when she found your panties in their room. Now who look like a hoe?" she shot back.

I stood there with my mouth open and for the first time, I felt embarrassed hearing about my past. After all this time, I had been tryna forget about that part of my life when I was letting men abuse my body, just because they said I was fine.

"That's the past and I'm past that. Look, I'm sorry it came out like that, but I didn't mean to judge you. It just caught a bitch by surprise because that's not you. You were always the one telling me if a man ever tries to fuck you in a club, he didn't really care about you and pussy was all he wanted."

"Yeah, I know, but this is different. Moe and I love each other, we're in love with each other. That's my man out there, my future husband and my friend. I didn't just meet him, we have chemistry, you feel where I'm coming from?" she asked, spilling her feelings about her man to me so I would understand.

We both stood there quietly searching our mind for something else to say, until I opened my mouth to tell her about my plans with Swift. We just looked at each other again before embracing in a hug, just as we heard a knock on the door.

Once we made it back to our table, we caught Moe and Swift with their eyes glued to two girls locking lips with each other. I knew men were all freaks and got a hard-on from girl-on-girl action, so I made my way towards both girls, just to give the club a show. Well, more so Swift, so he'd know what he got coming tonight. I had never so much as touched a girl sexually before, so the whole club could tell a bitch was nervous and on the other hand, I didn't want to fall weak and get addicted to pussy, because the world knew how much power it held. It could easily turn the best of friends into enemies.

The closer I got to the two girls locking lips, the more I recognized the one with her back towards me, but I couldn't tell if that was her for sure until she turned around.

"Girl, where you going?" I heard Tay ask, but I never broke my stride. I was committed and didn't think I'd ever have the courage to try something like this again. While Post Malone was congratulating me for finally growing a backbone to try something new, my heart literally skipped a beat.

I heard bitches screaming, "Double B's," from almost every direction. I quickly drew my gun, thinking about the promise I made to my sister about not giving a bitch the chance to trick me out my life and that's when she turned around.

Staring me in the face was E'mani, the bitch who killed my sister. I was really looking forward to this and I was always ready to make a move when a muthafucka got my timing wrong. So, without hesitation I aimed and fired twice, watching as both bullets met their target, knocking her body to the floor. Like an alarm sounding off, everybody started panicking and screaming, trying to make it out the front door without being hit by a bullet meant for somebody else.

It was like a stampede and with every second that passed, I swear I felt like everything was moving in slow motion. I had a feeling it was my time to meet the creator and I was willing to accept mine like a boss bitch, because I got who I wanted. I searched for Tay while screaming her name and began to panic when I couldn't find her. I looked around until my eyes started playing tricks on me and I thought I was seeing Mahogany.

I knew it couldn't be her because I killed that bitch, but the hot slugs entering my chest told me different. I tried to fight but my lungs wouldn't, and as Mahogany stood over my body, all I could think about was breaking my promise to Shanel, before multiple bullets riddled my body.

Chapter 11

Mahogany

"What the fuck!" I shouted as I repeatedly hit the steering wheel while weaving in and out of traffic. I had no feelings at the time, so I didn't care about the fuckin police, I didn't care about the fucking red light and I damn sure didn't care about the fucking stop signs, I had to get my girl to the damn hospital before she bled to death. Champagne and Passion held a shirt over her stomach to stop the blood from pouring out, but it wasn't working, because she was bleeding all over my fucking car.

"I can't fucking believe this shit! How the fuck did that bitch get in the club without anyone of us knowing?" I shouted again to no one. I was more so thinking out loud. I knew the bitch would come try E'mani after she thought she killed me, but how did she know E'mani was home?

"Mahogany, I need you to drive a little faster, it looks like she going unconscious," Champagne said as she repeatedly slapped E'mani across the face to keep her from going to sleep. I was afraid to look back there due to the fact that if she did die, I didn't want the reason to be because I was tryna be nosy and didn't make it to the hospital in time. So, I applied more pressure to the gas pedal.

My thoughts quickly went back to CoCo and why she wanted to kill E'mani and me. *What was she going through to make it come down to killing her sisters? Why?* I couldn't come up with a legitimate answer if my own life depended on it, so I focused on my sister, once I heard her scream from the pain. We pulled up to the ER and I swear it was like a zoo in there. People were everywhere, tryna get the attention of a doctor to take care of their own emergencies.

"We need a doctor right now, my sister has been shot and she's losing a lot of blood," I said to the first person we saw behind the receptionist desk when we walked in.

"Well ma'am, you're not the only one who needs a doctor in here and you're not the wife or mistress of the president of the United States. So, just like everybody else, you need to take a ticket and wait for your number to be called or—" I guess the sight of Champagne in her face, getting ready to go off like a ticking time bomb was enough to make the bitch get her mind right, because all of a sudden she resembled a child being chastised.

"I don't give a damn about everybody else in here. My sister needs a fucking doctor now and if you don't do your fucking job and make that happen in the next two seconds, I promise you really gone regret it. Because if she dies, everybody in this bitch dying with her." The whole lobby went quiet as they couldn't help staring at us, because after all the crazy gun violence going on nationwide, people were starting to take threats very seriously.

About two seconds later, a doctor and three nurses came running to take E'mani away. Champagne, Passion and I waited in the lobby, thinking about all the shit a black person had to go through to get help. We always had to literally show our ass and act ghetto for a muthafucka to respect us and the world wonders why we're always so angry.

I called Rue to tell him what happened before dialing E'mani's mother, which I really didn't wanna do, because I knew this was like déjà vu to her. This was the second time she had been called to the hospital in a year because E'mani had been shot, but she needed to know. She showed up about an hour later and to my surprise, she explained to me in tears that E'mani hadn't spoken to her in two months. It was fucked up that E'mani didn't even tell her mother she had beat the murder charge and had been released, but I really couldn't judge her because I was on the outside looking in, and didn't know her reason for doing so.

I sent Champagne and Passion home without introducing them to Mrs. Newman for one reason. They both looked exactly like your typical ghetto fabulous hood bitches, with them long ass Cardi B press-on fingernails, and I didn't need Mrs. Newman judging them. I stayed a couple more hours until E'mani came out of surgery and then her mother forced me to go home to get some rest. Sleep was the last thing on my mind at the moment and I really needed me a cigarette because a bitch nerves were fucked up.

I left the hospital in a hurry and just drove until I found myself at the cemetery staring at my sisters' gravesites. Deep down inside, I kinda felt like shit for killing CoCo and wanted to confess to Shanel, but at the same time I felt my hand had been forced and I did what anybody in my situation would do. Loyalty ain't promised, but throughout my whole life other than love, that's all I've ever wanted from anybody. I guess I'm cursed because all I seemed to attract was people who are brilliant at the game of deception which always caused me grief.

Why was my life so fucked up? I wanted to know but couldn't seem to make sense of anything. I yelled at the top of my lungs asking God why, on the verge of tears until the crunchy sound of falling leaves being crushed under somebody's feet caused me to draw my gun.

"Who's out there?" I shouted, slowly making my way to my car. It was so dark. I couldn't even see my hand in front of my face, until gunfire that didn't belong to me lit up the night. *Shit!* I wanted to yell as I heard the whistling sound of bullets flying past my head, before I finally fired a shot back to let them know I was also strapped.

Scared as I was, I was determined to make the short distance to my car without getting hit and getting the hell out of here. Once I did start the car, I applied so much pressure to the gas pedal, the whole car felt like it was floating when it got to moving. I had to find somewhere safe I could go, because my gut was screaming that they were still behind me. I back tracked and headed towards the hospital at about 60 mph, before I came up with an idea at the last minute and made a quick detour.

"Please answer! Please answer!" I chanted as I picked up my phone to call Rue. on the third ring he answered but never had a chance to say anything before I told him what was going on. "Baby, somebody's tryna kill me!" I shouted, out of breath before continuing. "I'm about two minutes from turning in your projects in my white Beemer and they're right on my ass. I need you to 'X mark the spot' behind me right now!"

I knew this was about to cause them to lose money tonight from the heat I was about to bring, but I really didn't give a damn, my life was more important. Soon as I turned in, I couldn't help but stare in surprise as I passed two men on every corner with masks covering their identities and Dracos in their hands. They all nodded their heads at me as if they were recognizing their queen's entrance and wanted to pay their respects.

I drove straight to the back where I met Rue standing in the parking lot before I heard war behind me, sounding like thunder and lightning repeatedly striking in the same area. Rue grabbed and hugged me into his arms while everything took place and I couldn't explain enough how safe he made me feel. The whole world knew I was a strong woman in a lot of ways and there wasn't too many things I couldn't handle, but today I was afraid. I was afraid I would die by the hands of somebody who's hurting and wanted revenge for me killing their friend or family. Being with Rue was really helping me to understand the value of life from the love he showed, and I didn't want to see him, Passion, or Champagne hurt because my past caught up with me.

"You alright?" Rue asked, staring me in the eyes as if he could look into my soul.

I stared back, not wanting to break eye contact while I answered, "Yes," but it was killing me, because I knew my eyes would reveal how vulnerable I felt and I didn't want him to see me so weak. He smiled before kissing my lips as I continued to stare, and at that point I was willing to give up my right arm to know what was going through his head.

"Baby, you have to learn to stop being so tough all the time and let me love you," he said, catching me off guard with his statement. His words really hit home because Supreme used to tell me that same thing. But how can I let somebody love me or love somebody, when I've never been taught how? My mother didn't even love me, and Supreme only taught me how to be his ride or die gangsta bitch. So, my struggles forced me to build this protective shield so nobody can never hurt me again.

I didn't respond because I didn't know what to say, all I could do was hold on to him, until he received a call that the car fled once the first two men started shooting. He looked at me as he was hanging up the phone and I just knew something bad had happened.

"Baby, do you know who was following you?" he asked in a stern tone. I hesitantly shook my head, but not before explaining to him everything that took place, from the time I left the hospital. I was forced to stay with Rue for the night, because he wouldn't have it any other way after I told him what happened.

We walked into his apartment and I was amazed, he actually had good taste to be a man. his living room was furnished with top-of-the-line patent leather couches, two chaises and an electric fireplace that could probably heat up any room within five minutes. The kitchen counters were all marble and in the corner by the dining room table was a fully loaded mini bar. While I was taking a tour of the rest of the place, R-Kelly's slow jams started playing from the surround sound speakers scattered around the place.

"How about a drink?" I asked, to steer things in another direction because I knew what was about to happen. It's not that I didn't want it to happen, because I did. I just get nervous when I'm around Rue, like it's my first time all over again.

He stood directly behind me and begun rubbing my shoulders before leaning to whisper in my ear, "Yeah, only if I can have you afterwards." I turned to look into his eyes and without a second thought, demanded him to kiss me as I got lost in his gaze. We undressed each other, before I took charge and laid him face down on top of the blanket he had on the floor. I then rubbed my hands down his body and licked his ears with my hot tongue. I could tell he was enjoying every second as he squirmed, moaned and rubbed his hardness against the floor.

"Cum for me, baby," I commanded before rubbing my nipples against his ass as I leaned over him, reaching to grasp his dick while kissing and biting his back. I traced my tongue down his spine, continuing over his ass and to his soft warm sack as I gently stroked his dick.

"Close your eyes," I told him firmly and kissed his lips, before running my tongue down his arms, chest and along his side while turning him over. I could feel him breathe heavily as I bit and nibbled on his stomach, then nuzzled the soft fur that surrounded his dick. Before I licked the wetness off the head, I gently teased his testicles with my nails. I loved driving him crazy with desire, and it was at that moment he demanded me to suck his dick. Unlike our first episode, this time I was ready and willing to please my man like a real golden head.

"How deep you want me to suck it?" I continued to tease him for my own enjoyment, but the joke was on me once he pumped his hips and forced his dick deep into the back of my throat.

"That deep!" he moaned. I sucked it to the base then back to the head, twisting and turning my hand around his dick with every in and out motion. He moaned loudly and passionately called my name. "Damn, Mahogany.... suck that dick, baby."

"You want this pussy?" I asked, already knowing the answer. After moistening my hand with lubricant, I glided my hand over his hardness, straddled him and slid all the way down until I was full. I wanted him to watch me cum as I forced him to stare into my piercing green eyes. He raised his hips to meet me halfway as I reached down to rub my throbbing clit. The feeling of him penetrating me while I pulled at my clit was more than I could handle, and I exploded.

Hot and still horny, I sucked him again while he rubbed my pussy, with hard but gentle strokes. I wanted to feel him inside me for a second time, but I guess he had other plans for us, as he gently laid me down on my back and spread my legs wide to where I was completely exposed. My clit hardened and began to throb again as his thick fingers entered me and came alive. He asked, "You like what I'm doing?" which turned me on even more and I completely lost control over my body as he had me almost speaking in tongues.

"Yes!" I cried. "Oh, yes! Eat me, baby. I need it." With that being said, he pushed his face in my hairless pussy, pressing his lips against mine. His tongue was hot and wet as it moved in and out of my slippery pussy. My juices ran out of my hole fast and heavy as he lapped them up while sliding one of his fingers deep inside me. I began humping my pussy against his face, begging him to fuck me hard as he slid another finger inside me.

"It feels so good, baby! Fuck me harder, it's coming!" While I was having one long-lasting orgasm, Rue licked my juices from his fingers, before lapping my pussy again. It didn't take him long to figure out what I wanted next and before I knew it, I was in my all-time favorite position, face down and ass up. He then positioned himself behind me and begun rubbing his dick up and down my dripping cave. I bucked my ass, loving the hard dick inside me, thrusting with so much force that I swore I felt it in my chest.

"Ahhhh... get this pussy, baby," I moaned, biting down on my bottom lip. I tried to stop all sounds from coming out of my mouth, not wanting him to get too cocky, but it was too late. He was putting it down so good, my voice betrayed me, and I started moaning my pleasure like never before as I came back-to-back. He moved in and out of me with a smooth motion, before picking up speed as the feeling got better with every stroke.

I was already in love with this man, but it was like he knew my body as if he owned it my entire life. Without warning, he slapped and squeezed my ass, bringing out the lioness in me. I kept pushing it out to let him know I wanted more, but he rolled me over onto my back, before reaching under my thighs and grabbing hold of my ass cheeks. At first I was surprised as he stood up, held me in his arms and began pumping into me, but always quick to adapt to any situation, I held onto his shoulders and wrapped my legs around his waist as I bounced up and down on his dick.

I got so excited I erupted in waves as my juices slowly dripped down our legs. My pussy tightened around his dick and he rushed me to the wall so we would have more support. Pictures and everything else in our way started falling to the floor as it felt like an earthquake hit, and within seconds of that happening, he exploded deep inside of me as we both came crashing to the floor.

Keith Williams

Chapter 12

Champagne

I've never been a real religious person, but I think we all appreciated the Almighty up above for sparing E'mani's life, even though she had to wear a colostomy bag. I still wanted to know what the hell was going through CoCo's mind to pull some shit like this, after everything they been through together. That shit was like committing treason and when you commit treason, you get exactly what that bitch CoCo got. Damn, I remember when I used to think you was real.

Mahogany sent Passion and me back to Gainesville until everything cooled down, while she stayed with E'mani. I wanted to protest, but I also knew now wasn't the time and besides, she was only doing what she thought was best for us, so we said our bye's and made our way to the car. We were both so fucking stressed, the minute we entered the car, our seats reclined as if the car had body sensors and knew we had a crazy ass day.

I was tired of the weight of the world on my shoulders, every time we relieved ourselves of one stressful situation, it seems another one showed its face. When will all this shit end? I wanted to scream. I really needed something to smoke like right now, and I guess God was feeling my pain or felt sorry for me because without warning, Passion pulled out about seven grams of loud so stank, it burned the hair on the inside of my nose. What was understood didn't need to be explained, so silence was all we heard as we started rolling up before fogging the windows once the blunt was lit, forcing us to forget about all our problems for the time being.

"Passion, do you realize how much we've changed since we met Mahogany?" I asked as I took a pull of the blunt. "I mean, shit real now. We even have dudes afraid of us, ain't that's some shit?" We both laughed, reminiscing about the time we went to handle business in Daytona Beach, Florida, and the nigga who was talking the most shit, ended up being the main one about to piss on himself when the bitch came out of us.

"Hell yeah, I realized that a while ago, but check this shit out. I been reading a lot of them urban books lately, where the females be taking over the city and running shit, and they don't even be living like that fa'real. I mean, they bust their guns, but any bitch can do that, like that bitch princess from *Deadly Reigns*. I wish I was in that book. I'll show that lil young bitch how a real thoroughbred do it, and that Latina bitch Angel from Dutch—"

"Hold up!" I said, putting my hands up to cut her off. "Now, you can't hate on Angel, she was a gangsta bitch fa'real. That's my girl right there and I wish I was in a book with her, we'd take over the whole damn world. But then again, that bitch a little too controlling for me and besides, I like dick. I don't need her tryna feed me fish." We both burst into laughter, feeling good and stress free from the Loud.

We were having such a good time talking and laughing with each other that we lost track of time and when I looked out the window, the sun was starting to rise. I finished the blunt before flicking the roach out the window and started the car to blind in with traffic. The temperature was cool for the most part as we crossed onto the interstate and feeling the effects of the Loud, mixed with Passion snoring, I caught myself staring at her as the day we met popped into my head.

Coming off summer vacation, it was Passion's and my first-time stepping foot in Gainesville High School. High school was like a fashion show, so it was all about who had the latest fashion and whose weave was the flyest, to determine if you would be popular or not. Now I can't lie, at the young age of fourteen, Passion was eye candy. Rocking her blue and white fitted Robin's Jeans, with the logo imprinted big on her back pocket. Her three-inch red bottoms went good with her Robin's fitted tee and a pair of RayBan sunglasses to top her outfit off. Her father was high ranking in the military at the time, so money wasn't an issue when it came to his little girl.

Me on the other hand, I had to boost most of my clothes from the malls and outlets to stay caught up with the latest fashions and designs that came out. My father turned into a drug addict by the time I was eight and my mother only had an eighth-grade education, so Burger King and McDonald's were the only jobs she could get to support us.

I mobbed down the school hallway like America's Next Top Model, on my way to the cafeteria to eat breakfast with my friends from middle school behind me. Being a loudmouth like always and not paying attention to my surroundings, I accidently bumped into Passion, causing her to spill food all over her new clothes. At first, I felt bad and was going to apologize, until I noticed she was wearing my entire outfit, from my red bottoms to my RayBan sunglasses. I knew Passion was angry because it showed in her face, but before she could say anything out of her mouth, I lashed out.

"Damn bitch, watch where the fuck you going!" I said, before walking off without looking back. The whole cafeteria laughed and while I was too busy running my mouth again, Passion picked up her breakfast tray, ran behind me and repeatedly knocked me upside the head while everybody just sat there and watched. Once the resource officer showed up, he found me laid out, unconscious in a pool of blood from my head.

I snapped back to reality, rubbing the back of my head and smiled at what I was just thinking about, before answering my ringing phone.

"Speak to me," I said before I listened and smiled because I knew that sexy voice from anywhere, and just the deepness of it made my panties feel like they had just got rained on from how moist they felt. Sweatt was spitting that thug passion shit to me. He and I had been secretly seeing each other behind Mahogany's back. Passion didn't even know and that's how I wanted to keep it.

I knew how close Mahogany and Sweatt's bond was, but I didn't care about all that. I'm grown, he grown, so why can't two grown muthafuckas do what they want, without somebody having something to say about it? I wanted to tell Mahogany anyway, it was Sweatt who didn't want me to. We talked for fifteen minutes without making it too obvious that something was up and then hung up, only after I agreed to do him a big favor.

"Passion," I said to get her attention. "It's time to do what we do best. Sweatt has a job for us and he said it needs to be done like yesterday. You know he gone make it worth our time."

Once I went over everything with Passion, I drove straight to a neighborhood by the name of Tree Top when we made it to the city limits of Gainesville. We were already turned up from the situation at the club with CoCo, so we were ready to handle business and get the fuck out of there, no bullshit. While Passion went to knock on the door, I waited behind the building where I couldn't be seen.

"Who is it?" I heard a woman shout. I'm guessing it was Shontae, Raw's girlfriend. Raw's the dude we were looking for. She quickly snatched open the door with an attitude but changed her demeanor when she saw Passion standing there.

"Can I help you?" Shontae asked with her face twisted with disgust. By me knowing Passion for so long, it wasn't hard to figure her out, so when a situation like this presented itself to have a little fun, I knew she would take it.

"Yes, you can help me. I would like to know if Raw live here?" Passion answered and asked. Now, I'm pretty sure Shontae felt disrespected by some woman showing up to her house asking about her man, but somehow, she stayed calm.

"Who the hell is you?"

"Well, if you must know, they call me Passion," she said before turning around to show off the tattoo on her lower back that spelled out her name. "But, I met Raw at the club where I dance and I don't usually come to my customer's houses like this, but he put that big dick on me so good the other night, I just had to find him. And then his head game had a bitch running up the damn walls fa'real." I couldn't help but laugh my ass off at how crazy Passion was, but she played her game like a pro and kelp her poker face on.

Shontae looked so mad, you could almost see the steam coming out of her ears, like a cartoon character. She looked as if she wanted to kill Passion before she started crying and quickly power walked towards her kitchen. Passion quickly stopped her with a blow to the back of the head with her .22, knocking her to the floor. I stepped in not too long after, still laughing before closing the door to the apartment.

"Damn girl, that bitch was about to go get something for your ass," I said to Passion as I stared at Shontae, before kicking her in the ribs a couple times while she held her side, moaning in pain. I can't lie, I loved the sound of a female moan. After watching Shontae beg for her life like the weak bitch she was, I tied her hands and feet to a chair.

"This is how it's gone go. Now, I really don't want to kill you. But I will, without thinking twice about it," Passion spoke while staring Shontae in her face. "We came here for your boyfriend. We know he's not here, because you would've been put your foot in his ass, when I told you how good he fucked me. So, what I'm going to do is call him from your cell phone and you're going to tell him something's wrong with your son and that you need him to come home right away."

She shook her head in agreement as the tears fell down her face. I just sat back on the love seat like a boss bitch and watched my girl Passion handle her business. She grabbed Shontae's cell, went through her contacts and found Raw's number, before pressing talk to call him.

"What's going on, baby, is everything okay?" Raw asked soon as he answered and heard the tone of her voice as if she had been crying.

"No! Ra'Shae has a bad fever and his body is on fire. He's been crying all day and it's driving me crazy. I've tried everything, but nothing seems to work, so I need you to come home right now so we can take him to the hospital," Shontae responded. Sweatt told me Raw's weakness was his bastard son. We knew he loved the little boy more than he loved himself and would feel responsible being that he was never home, so the plan was to make him feel guilty as possible. Raw told Shontae to stay there and wait for him before she did anything, then hung up.

It took him less than fifteen minutes to get home and when he walked into the house, he had one hell of a surprise waiting for him.

I stood behind the door and soon as Raw entered, he was met by the butt of my snub nose .357 to the back of his head, knocking him unconscious. While I grabbed him up off the floor and tied him to a chair next to Shontae, Passion stood on the other side of her, not saying a word. I slapped him a couple times, waking him up to the reality of his fate.

"What the fuck! Who the fuck are y'all and what you doing in my house?" Raw shouted in a slurred tone. Passion and I just looked at him before shaking our heads, because we knew he had no idea what he'd gotten him and his family into.

"Listen, pretty boy!" I said, getting face-to-face with him. "I know you don't know who we are, but I want to let you know, you've fucked over the wrong nigga. In this game of life, you gotta know how to choose your moves a little wiser and think about whose lives you're putting at risk." Raw looked at Shontae, seeing that she was in a state of shock, then instantly thought about his son.

"Where the fuck is my son, bitch?" he shouted, spitting hatred everywhere. The way Passion was looking, I knew she felt disrespected and when she felt like that, it was no telling what her crazy ass would do. Within the blink of an eye, she stepped to Raw, forcing her .22 into his mouth.

"Now who's the bitch? You know, you have a real disrespectful ass mouth. They don't call me Passion because I'm sweet, and I'm really getting tired of your mouth, so what we need you to do is run that money you owe Sweatt, or your bitch will see you do more than just suck on my shit."

Shontae quickly frowned her face up at Raw. I guess when she heard the words owe and Sweatt in the same sentence, she knew Raw had gotten them into some bullshit.

"Sweatt sent some hoes to do his dirty work for him. Well, how I see it, y'all going to have to kill me and—"

"No, Raw! Just give them the money so they can leave," Shontae shouted, stopping him before he could finish his sentence. I stood in the kitchen leaning against the counter watching how Raw played the role of a gangsta, not once thinking about his family. I then walked to the lower cabinet, pulled out a deep-frying pan and filled it with Crisco before sitting it on the stove. Once I did that, I turned the stove on before walking into the bedroom.

I was through with the bullshit and really felt as if he thought we were some kind of joke, but in a matter of seconds he quickly realized the joke was on him, when he noticed me walking back into the kitchen with their five-month-old baby, before holding him over the now frying Crisco threatening to drop the little bastard.

"This what you wanted, ha? Where the fuck is the money or I swear, I'll fry this little muthafucka right now!"

"Please! Not my baby, please!" Shontae begged over and over as Raw stared, trying to blink back his own tears.

I held the baby inches from the pot and was seconds from letting go, until Shontae screamed, "There's two black bags of money in a hole behind the refrigerator." *A woman was always the weak link, especially when there were kids involved,* I thought as I shook my head before sitting the baby down on the couch.

Passion helped me rock the refrigerator and after the fourth try, we finally pushed it over spilling everything inside. Like Shontae said, there were two bags in the hole and once Passion quickly made sure they were full of money, I sent a single shot to both Raw and Shontae's heads, ending their struggles of being parents.

Passion and I then went around wiping down everything we touched with bleach, before grabbing the baby and the money and walking out the door. I had no intention of keeping the little bastard, but at the same time, it wasn't in me to kill a baby either. So, while Passion started the car and drove around the building, I sat the baby on the steps of a neighbor, rang the doorbell and ran back to the car as if I was competing in the Olympics for a gold medal in track and field.

Keith Williams

Chapter 13

E'mani

I awoke to the sight of my mother sound asleep in the chair next to my bed. Her face was all puffy and swollen around the eyes, so I could tell she had been crying, but that was the least of my worries. I wanted to know why the hell she was even here. I had nothing to say to her because she showed me months ago where her loyalty lies. I'm her daughter for Christ's sake and she abandoned me like old underwear that had shrunk two sizes from being washed too many times.

I let my eyes roam around the room as if I was a baby just being born into this world, until they landed on my stomach. *I can't believe CoCo really shot me*, I thought as I fingered the bandages that kept me from bleeding to death. She actually looked me in the eyes before shooting me down like a bum ass bitch in the street.

"Double B's," I whispered to myself, now wondering how much the word really meant to the women who screamed it. It seems lately it had no value to it, because there was no trust, and I felt the need to find a way out before I ended up like so many others, dead and in jail.

My mother couldn't seem to find a comfortable position as she slept, because she tossed and turned every couple of minutes. I wanted to wake her so we could talk, but then again, I really didn't want to hear her excuses to why she treated me the way she did, so I just stared. I stared at the wrinkles in her face and the bags under her eyes. My mother had aged so much in the last four months, it kind of scared me.

"Ma!" I said, a little louder than I should have. I wanted to make sure she would hear me over the dream she was having as she slept. She scrambled before opening her eyes, just as I was about to call her again.

"E'mani!" she said excitedly. "Baby, I'm so sorry, please forgive me for the—"

"Ma, stop it!" I raised my voice to cut her off, so she could hear me over her own voice. She got quiet and for a long minute, we both just stared at each other until the occult silence got the best of me. I loved my mother more than anything in this world, even though at times I wanted to hate her. She was the only person I had left that I could truly say wants the best for me, so I felt I had to make things right between us, in case something happened and it's too late.

"Ma, I have something to tell you, so can you please let me get it out before you say anything. I don't want your excuses and I don't want your apologies. I want you to hear what I have to say." I stopped her for a minute to look her in the eyes and make sure we were on the same page. She stared back without saying anything and that encouraged me to continue.

"I wanted to hate you so much for the way you left me, I wanted to see you suffer and I was also close to wishing you were the one deceived, instead of my father. Ma, you really hurt me and abandoned me at a time I needed you the most. At first, I didn't think you should be here but as I thought about it, you're the only person I have that loves me and I would hate myself if something happened, without us getting past this." We were both crying at this point and I didn't really mean to lash out on her like I did, but sometimes trying to be honest without being brutal is like trying to swim without getting wet.

She apologized while wiping away her tears, even though I told her earlier I didn't want to hear it. We hugged, cried some more and then she told me Mahogany was the one who called her, but she sent her home because she felt Mahogany was to blame for all the mishaps in my life within the last year.

I told her it wasn't fair to blame Mahogany because I was a grown woman and knew right from wrong, even though in the back of my mind, I knew my mother was right and felt the same way she felt.

"Oh yeah, baby, before I forget. Some lady has been coming to see you for the last couple days saying she wanted to talk to you when you woke up. She told me her name, but I can't seem to remember at the moment. I'll see if I can find her business card in my purse," explained my mother as she dug into her handbag in search of the business card from this mystery woman. I thought hard while I watched her, as if she was on a treasure hunt, but couldn't seem to think of any person in particular. She knew damn near everybody I knew, so if she couldn't remember, that meant it was somebody I've never met.

She was in full Sherlock Holmes mode as she found it, and at that exact moment Mahogany came walking in, causing Mama to wave the card in the air at me and mouth, "I'll show you later," while rolling her eyes.

Mama was really starting to hate Mahogany's guts and didn't mind showing it. I slightly laughed when she excused herself, and once she was out of earshot, Mahogany let me know she noticed my mother's dislike of her.

"I see Mrs. Newman made up her mind that I would be the one taking the blame for all the bullshit going on in her daughter's life?" stated Mahogany as she raised her eyebrows and gave me a look, like she knew I had been telling my mother creepy stuff about her. I eyed her back, because the bitch was going crazy. Out of all people, she should know by now how my mother was and besides, E'mani don't be on that two-faced shit. A couple minutes into our little stare down, she made herself comfortable in the chair next to my bed, before changing the subject like she wasn't just feeling some type of way about my mother. But I laughed and brushed it off as her feeling guilty, because she knew I was authentic.

"Anyway, how you been feeling? I hope these doctors hurry up and get you right, because that stank ass shit bag do not look cute," she said as she moved my colostomy bag to the side, so she could make room for herself next to me on the bed. I damn near pushed her ass on the floor, because we both knew she was making fun of my situation, but I gave her a pass because I was still feeling kind of weak. Show me a bitch on this universe that could make a colostomy bag look cute, and I'll drop down to the floor and kiss her feet like she's royalty.

"Watch your mouth about my colostomy bag, because without this bitch I'll be shittin on your ass right now," I shot back. She frowned up her face like she was disgusted and I laughed as I continued, "I'm doing better though. Mama and I had a heart-to-heart right before you walked in, and we both decided to leave the past behind us. But I would like to know, why am I always the one getting shot?" I looked her in the eyes before lifting my gown a little so she could see the bandages that covered my war wound.

She ignored my question without even attempting to speak on the subject, as she slowly ran her hand across my stomach as if I was some kind of science project, she was seeing for the first time. I hated the look she had on her face because I knew she was feeling sorry for me and that's not what I wanted. I didn't need her sympathy or anybody else's for that matter, but at that moment, guilt hit me like a blow from Mike Tyson and I felt I needed to tell her the truth.

"I know why CoCo shot me," I started, really not believing I was confessing to something I promised myself I would take to my grave. I could tell I had Mahogany's attention, so I couldn't punk out now, but I was seconds from doing just that.

"She shot me because I killed Shanel. What you didn't know was that Shanel was like CoCo in more ways than you thought. She was going to kill me, but somehow God was with me and I got her first. CoCo thought she knew, because you two left Shanel and me in the car that day, so she wanted revenge." I looked up at Mahogany and I could tell she was in deep thought, but the silence was killing me, because I needed to know what was on her mind.

"She must have thought I had something to do with it or that I knew what happened, because just the other day she showed up to the house and tried to kill me. She shot and killed Rue's sister instead, and this whole time I thought she was just hurt, because she lost her other half, but she felt betrayed that somebody she considered a sister killed her twin," she spoke, while at the same time trying to put all the pieces together to this crazy ass puzzle.

I felt bad that it all had to come down to this, but I don't regret what I did because Shanel's ass would've killed me if she had the up's, so I'm not hearing none of that shit Mahogany talking about. The room got quiet again and the occult silence was driving me crazy because I didn't know what was on Mahogany's mind. She could be a shiesty bitch when she wanted to be and I'll hate to have to put one in her head, because she thought I was wrong and wanted to judge me herself.

"Mahogany, our bond could never be broken, it's Double B's 'til the death for me," I said to see where her head was, and I could tell she saw right through me.

"Bitch!" she responded as she laughed. "You know you scary as hell, but everything good. I'm still screaming Double B's until my lungs hurt." Neither of us had anything more to say on the subject, so we dropped it. I knew things would never be the same after the shit I just confessed, and I felt that was even more motivation to separate myself from the Baller Babies. Mahogany's phone rang taking over attention away from our own thoughts and I just stared at her, reminiscing on the good times we've had, like when I let her talk me into doing a stripper dance in Doe Boy's club for his birthday.

Mahogany and I stood around the dressing room, talking and joking before we hit the stage. We were both half-naked with ass everywhere. I was sporting a black lace bra and panties, while Mahogany sashayed in her red see-through boy shorts and bra. I really wasn't feeling this shit and it wasn't me to show off myself half-naked like this, but Mahogany kept challenging me like I was green, so I had to prove to her that I wasn't green as she thought.

"Mahogany! E'mani! Get ready, y'all up next," a girl by the name of Fantasy shouted as she entered the dressing room from the stage.

The DJ had Adina Howard and Jamie Foxx's, "T-shirt and Panties" flowing through the loudspeakers as I walked onto the stage in a seductive stride, grabbing the pole and bending all the way over towards my spectators. The plan was to out-do Mahogany while I had the chance and I was ready. I then slowly walked around the pole, showing off my assets before climbing to the top, blowing a kiss to the crowd and then slowly sliding down into a split, while twerking to the beat. The club went crazy as money flew from every direction onto the stage and that was Mahogany's cue, so she slowly sashayed onto the stage, picked her victim then stared him down with her seductive, feline green eyes. The lights from the stage made her skin shine, so it looked as if she was glowing, and without hesitation she grabbed the pole, pulling herself up halfway before flipping upside down as she spread her legs apart until she resembled a capital "T." Our heads now inches apart, Mahogany winked at her victim before looking down at me. I was in a zone all on my own as I licked my full lips and followed suit, looking up into her eyes and within seconds, our lips were connected like two magnets.

While I slid my tongue inside her mouth, I raised my hands overhead and unhooked her bra, watching as it fell to the floor exposing her breasts. The club really went bananas once I stood to my feet and grabbed hold of her boy shorts as she slid out of them, down the pole and in between my legs.

Mahogany, now completely naked with her legs agape towards our audience, then slid her hands inside my panties with a swift and quick motion, pulling them down as I bent over and grabbed my ankles. We were both giving the club a view they would forever remember. The entire club went into an uproar as every man in there tried to put their bid in on us at the same time.

"E'mani!" Mahogany yelled, bringing me out of my trance. "I have to go, but no matter what, our bond could never be broken, remember that." We hugged for a long minute, then she got her stuff and left. I lay in bed and just stared at the ceiling, welcoming the silence after dealing with Mahogany. I really didn't know what I was gone do with my life. I had no plans, no goals and no way of knowing how to play the hand life had dealt me.

To keep from stressing too much about everything I've been going through, I decided to look at the darkness behind my eyelids. Yeah, I was on my way to sleep, tryna chase the dream of me getting my freak on, being that I still haven't gotten my kitty scratched since I've been home.

I was sleep for all of ten minutes before I felt the presence of a well-dressed woman that looked as if she could be the twin sister of the actress Meagan Good. She had caramel-colored skin, long jet-black hair and a shiny gold badge that made me well aware this visit was not one I was going to enjoy.

"Good afternoon, Ms. Newman. I'm Agent Watson with the Federal Bureau of Investigation and I would like to ask you a couple questions, if you don't mind?" she stated, showing me her FBI identification.

I answered, "No," as I sat up, but found myself feeling a little embarrassed when I caught her facial expression at the sight of my colostomy bag. I covered it with my blanket after a couple seconds and then cleared my throat to let her know she could start asking her questions.

"Ms. Newman, we're after your friend Mahogany White, the leader of the notorious gang run by women called the Baller Babies. We have been investigating Ms. White since she orchestrated the murder of Jermaine Watson, known on the streets as Supreme. We know she's smart, which is part of the reason we haven't caught her in the act, but she's not untouchable." She stopped just for a minute as she pulled out numerous of pictures from a folder. I looked on in shock as I realized how real this was. She had pictures of everybody: Mahogany, Nah Nah, Nicole, CoCo, Shanel, Kayla, me and even Champagne and Passion.

"We know she doesn't trust anybody because everybody she deals with ends up dead. Here's a picture of Supreme's deceased body, he was the first to die. Next, we have Shawn Ross, who was known on the streets as Doe Boy. I guess she had help with that one, because his bouncers died in the club with him, execution-style. After that, there was Supreme's little sister, Ja'mya and her lover Kayla, who was once Ms. White's friend. Oh, and my favorite one, which you probably know as Shay, she was Ms. White's blood cousin. I don't know why she would kill her, but she needs to be off the streets and we're asking for your help."

I was still focused on the pictures which she claimed were the work of Mahogany's work, when what she said next almost made my heart stop beating on me.

"It looks like you're having a hard time thinking about whether you want to help us or not. Well, here's a little something I guarantee will help you make the right decision," she stated as she pulled out more pictures of dead bodies. "You should be familiar with this one, being that you put the work in yourself. His name is Neeko Carter and you shot half of his face off, because he shot you and tried to kidnap you.

"Or what about these? They're unrecognizable because you had the house burnt to ashes, but this is my father, Judge Lester Wright and these are my sisters, Ashlyn and Alice Wright. Yeah, you heard me correct. They're my family and you had them killed. But, like I said before, I'm giving you the opportunity to help us get Ms. White, because I want the person who literally turned my life upside down, but I will get you if I have to."

If I was a man, I would say this bitch really had me by the balls and I honestly didn't know what to do. Mahogany was my girl and had risked her life for me many times. Loyalty wasn't just a word, it's our way of life, but God knows I didn't want to spend the rest of my life in prison. Agent Watson knew this also, that's why she continued provoking me until I gave her what she wanted, which was my word that I would help her take down my best friend and my ride or die bitch, Mahogany.

Chapter 14

Mahogany

I was so drained when I left E'mani at the hospital that once I got home, sleep was calling my damn name. Yeah, I was just that exhausted, physically and mentally. Then on top of that, the last couple hours kept flashing in my head. There was always some type of bullshit going on and somehow, I'd find myself slap dead in the middle of it all. It seemed to never fail, and I was damn near worn out.

That shit E'mani confessed about Shanel now had me questioning my judgement of the bitches I called family and that's not good, because how I see it, every bitch was suspect from now on. Word had now gotten around that CoCo shot E'mani and then I killed CoCo, so it's said the Baller Babies now had smoke with each other.

I laughed every time I overheard people whispering about it, because they blamed me for always wanting to be the boss of something and telling bitches what to do. But I couldn't care less what another bitch thought, long as they never brought that shit to my face. Otherwise, they could get the same thing CoCo's backstabbing ass got, period!

I stumbled into the house, but for some strange reason, I wasn't tired as I thought I was. I continued to my room anyway and as I was passing Shanel's, something kept telling me to go in. I really didn't know why, but I had a good feeling it was because of that shit E'mani told me about her being like CoCo in more ways than I thought, and that shit still didn't sit too well with me.

We still hadn't cleared her room, so everything was exactly how she left it and the moment I stepped through the door, I swear I could feel her spirit all around me. I turned to my right, before quickly turning to my left after hearing the door slam hard from the strong wind outside the open window. I was so damn jittery and I knew it was Shanel tryna warn me to get the fuck out of her shit, but I was committed and didn't have any intentions of leaving until I found what I was looking for. Whatever that is.

I went through every drawer and shoebox I saw, before I literally cursed Shanel's ass out for not warning me that I was about to touch her nasty ass black dildo, the one she called "Nasty for me." Well, at least that's what it had written in white ink down the side of it. I laughed after the initial shock, because she used to walk around like the rest of us were whores when we talked about dick, but this long and thick ass dildo proved she was more of a dick junkie than any of us.

I continued my search, now moving to the closet where I stumbled up on a mini, safe-like box that couldn't be opened without a key. I picked it up, noticing the weight before finding my way to the kitchen and abandoning the rest of my search altogether.

Now, I wasn't the smartest bitch in the world, but I had a feeling I didn't have to be to know Shanel's sneaky ass was hiding something. I grabbed the butter knife out of the side drawer, then proceeded to put my breaking and entering skills to use. It took me a little longer then I thought to open it, but once the contents were visible, all I saw was my life flashing before my eyes. It was like I was seeing the future of me going to prison for the rest of my life and somebody killing me. Shanel really had us all fooled and I would have never thought in a million years that she would be the one trying to bring the Baller Babies down. Damn, that bitch tricked me.

I pulled the items out one at a time, starting with the one I thought for sure would end our careers if it got into the wrong hands, which was a DVD. Not just any DVD, the one I told that bitch to destroy, the one I told her I never wanted to see again. The one she told me she would handle it, the one we took from Doe Boy's club, Magic City, the day we murdered him and his bouncers.

But I mean, why would she not destroy it, didn't that bitch know if she would've turned the DVD in, her stupid ass would've gotten life right along with the rest of us? Dumb bitch. I shook my head, because I really couldn't understand her motive. What was she going to do with it?

The next thing that caught my eye was the manila envelope with the words, "Got you," in bold print written on the front. I was really praying and hoping E'mani and I was wrong about Shanel, but something in the back of my mind was screaming otherwise. *Please prove me wrong, Shanel. Please*, I thought, as I opened the envelope and retrieved the content from inside.

I went through it, curious of what I might see and laughed out loud when I recognized myself on my knees, taking Doe Boy's manhood deep into my mouth. The next couple photos were of me and Hollywood or me with other men and in each one, my goodies were exposed. I mean, I was far from shy, but was this bitch obsessed with seeing my fat ass pussy? And the only thing these prove is that I love sex. Tell me what bitch didn't.

I was coming up on the end of the pictures and I was ready to toss the whole stack to the side, when the last five caught my attention, causing me to double take. I couldn't believe the betrayal when I finally focused on the pictures. I mean, I was more shocked then angry, but then I laughed because I should've seen this coming years ago.

CoCo, Shanel and Nicole were all naked in a small orgy, looking like they were fighting over Supreme's dick as he sat with his back against the headboard like he was really enjoying himself. The only two bitches in my crew missing were Nah Nah and Kayla, but I wasn't giving their asses the benefit of the doubt, because I know they were there too, who the fuck was taking the pictures! The last four I took my time slowly browsing through, as photos of Supreme with his dirty dick inside each one of them nasty ass bitches.

I felt so betrayed that I wish I could bring them hoes back to life and then kill their asses myself. But, I knew that was my fault, because I was the one who introduced them bitches to Supreme when we all graduated from the Florida Institution for Teenage Girls, and him pulling up in his Benz truck did nothing but make them thirsty bitches want him even more.

I remember Sweatt used to tell me all the time that loyalty ain't promised to nobody and at the time, I didn't want to hear it. But, as I think about it now, everybody I showed loyalty to showed me he was right. My luck was so fucking bad that it could be raining dicks outside right now, but soon as I step out, I'll get slapped right in the face with a fat pussy. What the hell have I done to deserve so much disloyalty?

I grabbed everything, putting it back into the box before carrying it out to the backyard. Without thinking twice, I dumped it all into the barbecue grill, dashed it with gasoline and then struck the match. I stood there and watched as the flames destroyed everything it came in contact with, still not feeling any better. I needed somebody to talk to, somebody I could tell how I felt and not have them judge me, or think I've gotten soft. I needed Rue.

I dialed his number and on the second ring, he answered, telling me he was on his way before hanging up. I ran into the bathroom for a quick shower because I knew where things were going to go and I wanted it. I was mentally and sexually frustrated. Once he showed up, just the look on his face told me he needed me as much as I needed him and that's where all communication ended, until we gave each other teeth-shattering orgasms.

"Bae, my life has been so fuckin complicated," I started pillow talking as I rested my head on his chest and listened to his heartbeat. "How can you know when a person will be disloyal in the end, when they've risked their life and even killed for you in the beginning?" I asked, not really expecting him to answer, but he was so much of a good listener that I poured out my heart, telling him everything that was on my mind. Even shit he wasn't supposed to know, which I regretted soon as it slipped out my mouth. He acted as if he was half asleep and didn't hear me, but I knew better. I was far from a dummy.

I woke the next morning to an empty bed and a note on my nightstand, it was a poem. I laughed as I read it, because it reminded me so much of E'mani and her little black book of poems she wrote about Supreme. I found it when I first moved in and then hid it in the kitchen drawer once I read it. Now that's one girl who was really in love with Supreme, but at the same time I can't talk, because at one point in my life, I was fucked up about his trifling ass as well.

I stretched my muscles before easing from underneath the comforter and squealed when the cool breeze of the morning tackled my naked body. I swear, I hated the winter season and would rather live my life without it, but hey, who was I to question Mother Nature. I grabbed my cell phone off the dresser before running to the bathroom. I low-key felt like a kid on Christmas morning, because we had not too long ago got the bathroom remodeled, and because of my crazy ass letting the sloppy body installation man smell the scent of my pussy up close, he installed six showerheads at my request without charging me. Now tell me that wasn't some wild ass shit. Who needs that many damn showerheads in one bathroom anyway, right?

Thirty minutes passed before I decided to get out the shower to get myself together. At times like this, I hated being in the house by myself. I had nobody to curse my ass out for no reason or for being the boss bitch I was. But at the same time, I loved it because I could walk around free as a bird, not one piece of garment on my body. Today, I decided a long black t-shirt would do as I ate a bowl of cereal and watched reruns of the show, *Black-ish*. I was coming up on the fifth episode and found myself laughing to the point of crying, when I heard Rue enter my house like he owned it.

I didn't know how he did it, but just looking at him turned me on and the thought of all the positions he had me in last night, only made it worse. I jumped up and leaped into his arms before wrapping my legs around his waist and showering his face with kisses. I didn't have on panties, so I know he felt the moisture from between my legs seeping through his shirt.

"Slow down, baby, damn I miss you too," he said, putting me down so I was now face-to-face with him. "Before I lose the courage to do it, I have something to tell you." I was now all ears, staring in his eyes and still trying to show him how horny I was.

"Baby, I really want this between me and you to work and by doing so, we have to be completely real with each other. Do you trust me?" he asked, staring back into my eyes but without the lust. It took me a couple seconds to answer, only because I didn't want him to know how much he really had me wrapped around his finger.

"Of course, I trust you. You've earned that much, but where is this coming from?" I wanted to know. Without even answering my question, he spoke again.

"Will you ride for me and stand strong for better or worse?"

"Yes, baby. I'll always be here for you, from the time the sun peep through the clouds, until the day you close your eyes permanently and even then, my love won't change," I replied, eager to know where all this was coming from. He turned away from me before walking towards the door, leaving me confused as I ever been. I stood there and just watched as he called out to whomever he had waiting outside for him because this shit was getting more confusing by the second. When two women entered my house, I automatically went to defense mode because there was now potential enemies in my territory.

"Do y'all trust me?" he spoke again now asking them the same questions while I stared back and forth at them. They answered almost the way I did, but more convincing.

"Okay, since you all trust me, what I want is for you to trust each other," he said, before stopping. I guess to catch my reaction before he continued, because I still said nothing. "Alexis, Brittany, this is my soon-to-be wife, Mahogany." I smiled like any bitch would, loving the upper hand I had over these bitches when he called me his wife.

"Mahogany, this is Alexis and Brittany. They are my business partners, but they also dance at Club Paid, which is where I met them a while ago. They're both in law school right now and should be graduating soon. They're real loyal girls."

I mugged him, ready to start illustrating on his stupid ass for even trying and disrespecting me by bringing some stripper hoes I know he'd been fucking into my house. Don't this nigga know I've been through this bullshit once before with Supreme? I'm the only bitch he needs. I'm more than enough for one nigga, so this wasn't going to work out, but before I could say anything, he stopped me.

"Now, you all know my motto. Loyalty is everything and your word is your bond. If you can't do what you say, how can you say what you'll do? You all said you trust me and will ride for me, well ride for us, because neither of you are going anywhere no time soon."

I couldn't take it anymore and excused myself to my bedroom to retrieve my purse, without saying a word. If I was soon to be that nigga's wife, then he should know me by now, and if he knew me, him and his two mutts better be out of my shit by the time I made it back to the living room. I smiled when I returned to find my living room not only bodyless, but the front door was left wide open to let me know they wasted no time putting some distance between them and the bitch who was about to end every last one of their careers.

Damn, just when I thought this nigga was the one to change a bitch's life, I thought as I went to throw on some clothes, before jumping in my car in search of some dick. To all the people in the world who was thinking about judging me right now, I really don't give a fuck because everybody needs something that can gives them peace at a time like mine, and I choose sex as my therapy.

Once my heart rate was back to normal and my hormones calmed down from going into overdrive, I kissed the guy next to me on the cheek and tiptoed to my car, so I could get home to call Champagne and Passion and tell my bitches about this shit.

Chapter 15

Champagne

I could tell Passion had never been to Sweatt's house, because she was stunned at how big it was, but who wouldn't be? That shit wasn't beautiful, it was breathtaking. I rang the doorbell as Passion and I carried the bags, and before I knew it, Sweatt was standing in front of us looking like a tall glass of water on a hot day, in a white wife beater and red gym shorts.

Upon entering his house, it was like you died and went to heaven, because everything was white as cocaine and looked like it was glowing. His thick, white chinchilla plush carpet was one of the most expensive things in there, at least that's what he claimed. So, before you entered, he always met his guests with a pair of white disposable house shoes. Once we received ours, we were led to the great room to talk business.

"Talk to me, let me know how everything went on your end," Sweatt wanted to know, eyeing the bags we had between our legs on the floor. He just looked so sexy to me and I literally had to catch myself on multiple occasions from trying to look at his dick through his shorts as I responded.

"Watch the news at eleven and you'll see we handled our business like always." Passion and I looked at each other, then smiled before slapping hands because that shit sounded too real. I then gave Sweatt the rundown, starting with the minute Passion knocked on the door and the little fun she had with Raw's girlfriend, Shontae.

Once our brief conversation was over, Sweatt mentioned the bags, noticing there were two. I guess he still didn't understand Passion and I were like bees to honey when it came to money. We dumped both bags out on the floor, then we'd started counting until we finished, or our fingers cramped up. Whichever one came first. We ended up with a little over eighty thousand, once we were done counting, which was a good piece of change for a nigga who stood on the corner like a stop sign.

Passion and I both knew Sweatt was in a good position financially, but we never expected him to tell us, that we could "Keep all the money for yourselves and thank you for taking care of everything."

That's some real boss shit and it really turned me on, which had me so ready to get some dick that I accepted his gesture, grabbed Passion's hand as she grabbed the money and headed for the car, so I could drop her ass off and double back.

Passion

Champagne was really acting suspicious as hell, the way she rushed away from Sweatt's house, but that bitch thought I didn't know what was going on. I saw the way she was looking at him. Her trifling ass wanted some dick. It was just fucked up how she was tryna hide it from me out of all people and then what put the icing on the cake was that I was home alone, while she was getting her freak on like we haven't done threesomes before.

I grabbed my cell, laid on the couch and scrolled through my contacts, looking for a night cap. I wanted somebody who could make my toes curl or make a bitch want to swallow his babies and crave the power of his dick, but nobody I came across could make me feel that way, so I dialed a number I hadn't used in a while as I got comfortable.

"You have reached the Hot Singles Chat Line. Press one to record your introduction," the automated system stated. I pushed one and soon as I heard the beep, I started recording. "Hi fellas, my name is Passion and I'm on here tonight, just looking for somebody to have a little fun with. I have a caramel skin complexion, I'm five-five, hair down my back and I'm thick in all the right places. I take pride in keeping my body in shape, so I'm speaking out to all the fellas. I'm not a chubby chaser, so if you're fat, please don't waste your time sending me messages. I'm calling from the Gainesville, Florida area, so if you're from my way and enjoyed what I had to say, hit me up and tell me about yourself."

Once I finished my introduction, I sat on the phone and just listened, thinking how desperate these men sounded to find a woman. After a while, I heard my phone beep and the automated system telling me I had three new messages. I pushed one to hear the first message before stretching my legs, because I knew I was in for a long night.

"What's good, Passion? Damn, you have a sexy ass name. But this ya boy Bullet Head and yes, I am a white boy, so I hope you don't mind kicking it with a male of another race. I have been dating black women for long as I can remember. Most white women don't have enough ass and that never turned me on.

"I'm six-one, ocean blue eyes and built like the actor, Vin Diesel. I feel where you're coming from on that comment about not sending you a message if we're fat. I feel the same way. I like to be able to pick a woman up in my arms and give her all of me during sex. I'm living in Gainesville right now and I'm really feeling you, so send me a message and let me know what's up, or maybe we could just chat one-on-one in the private room."

The white boy sounded too sexy and even though I liked men chocolate, I was willing to try something new. But at the same time, I wanted to hear from the other men before I made my decision. So, I pushed the number two button to hear that second message.

"You say your name is Passion? Well, all my friends call me Dolla and I'm five-ten, dark skin with dreads down to my chest. I have all my teeth and I don't smoke. I really think it's very unattractive for a person to do. I'm attending school at the University of Florida, studying to become a sex therapist and right now, I'm living on campus. I really love your voice and would like to get to know you, so message me back. You never know, this could be the beginning of a blessing to come."

I was too surprised to hear all that Dolla had going for himself. I could use a nigga like him, he had a good head on his shoulders and a promising future at satisfying me with perfection. In my mind, I already knew I would choose him but I still wanted to hear the last message, so I pushed three and listened.

"What's poppin, Passion? Dis ya boy Raymo and I liked what I heard, so that mean I want you and I always get what I want, no question about it. I'ma brown-skinned nigga with six golds gracing the top row of my mouth and tatted up like the subway in Harlem. I love eating pussy, I'm addicted to eating ass and I promise, I could make your pussy talk to me like never before. So yeah, you could say I'm a freak. I'm five-nine, and a hundred-eighty pounds. I live on the west side of Gainesville in a neighborhood called Phenix. Send me a message, so we can make something out of nothing."

That last message had me so wet and ready to break the screen on my iPhone to message him back, because he sounded like he could give me what I was looking for. I knew I should be picking Dolla, but after feeling the throbbing sensation between my legs, my fingers slipped and pushed buttons number three and then one, to catch up with Raymo. I told him my sister had my car so I couldn't go anywhere, and I just wanted to have a little phone sex. He was cool with that, then I sent him my number with intentions of having multiple orgasms like I knew Champagne was having.

Not even two minutes after I ended the call, Cardi B started rapping about "Money," as my phone rang.

"Dis Raymo," he said, soon as he heard my voice asking who was calling.

"What's up, Raymo? I'm just lying in the bed watching this porno starring Mr. Marcus' old ass. He don't be playing, he still be fucking the shit out of them girls," I responded, lying through my teeth, but I knew it was a good way to get things going. Like always, I was right, but he shocked me with how familiar he was with porno movies when he asked if I was watching Mr. Marcus fuck Cherokee.

"Naw, he giving all that dick to Super Head and I can't front, she taking it like a champion. You should see how she throwing it back and at the same time, begging him to go deeper. Damn, this shit getting me so wet." I knew he was probably grabbing at his dick, thinking he ran into a real deal freak. For the most part he was right, but really didn't know how ready I was to unleash it.

"Slide your panties off for me," he told me in his smooth voice. "Then, I want you to play with your clit until you cum, without sticking a finger inside your pussy." I did as I was told and knew he could hear the soft moans I was letting out.

"Ohh, that feels so good... Mmmm, I need something hard inside me," I responded, biting down on my bottom lip. He then said something about wanting the whole world to hear me pleasuring myself before I was to be penetrated. I begged and begged, but he wasn't having it.

"Keep going for me and put the phone down there so I can hear how wet you are." I rubbed my clit a little faster as I continued to follow his demands. I knew it was like music to his ears when he heard the sloppy sound of my wet pussy, before the main event of my approaching orgasm.

"Oh, I'm cumming! Ahhhh! Shit yeah, my pussy is so fuckin wet," I yelled as I came, being a little more extra than I really needed to be. "That felt so damn good, I have never cum so hard from my own hands. You really know how to bring the freak out a bitch, but I want to keep going. I want to cum until I can't cum no more, and my body feels so weak that I just lay here and can't move." The whole time I was giving him the blueprint of what I wanted, I had my phone between my legs, tryna capture the perfect angle of my swollen wet pussy lips before sending it to him.

"Damn, you have a fat pussy," he responded, complimenting my lady part. "Now, I want you to slide two of your fingers inside, before moving them in and out in a circular motion like you did your clit." Like the obedient bitch I was, once again I did what I was told, and my pussy opened so wide that I'm pretty sure he heard my fart from the air going in and out with my hand motion. I slightly laughed to keep myself from feeling embarrassed before soft moans took over.

"Put another finger in for me, but I want you to go slow and enjoy every stroke." I was slowly enjoying every stroke like he said, but my pussy was so sensitive that I automatically started breathing heavy, giving away that I was approaching another orgasm. He told me to keep going while instructing me to add another finger to the party, but I couldn't hold back the feeling of my earth-shattering release.

"Haaaa... Yes, baby! Fuck! Fuck! Fuck!" I screamed so loud that my lungs were starting to hurt. I was so weak and tired, I couldn't cum again if I wanted to. The two orgasms back-to-back like that wore me the hell out. We talked for a little while longer until we both got sleepy. I told him I really enjoyed myself and we said our good nights then hung up the phone, but not before giving him a little something to remember me by. I sent another picture of my legs spread wide as an eagle's wings, with two of my fingers separating my pussy lips.

The next morning, Champagne woke me up with the biggest smile on her face as she pulled the curtains open to bring light to my darkened room. She then gave me the rundown of what happened with her and Sweatt, before telling me she had a really big cake baked for him and then looked at me if to ask what I got into last night. Now, I know there is nothing wrong with having phone sex and pleasuring yourself with a man you met on a chat line. But there was no way I was telling Champagne a complete stranger made me tap out last night without even touching me, no fucking way.

Instead, I made up a lie about watching the movie *Baby Boy* all night until I fell asleep. I could tell she knew I was lying, but then again what I said was believable, so I guess she decided to let it ride. We went back and forth for another ten minutes, until she told me to take a shower and get dressed because we had somewhere to be. "Champagne, do you think these shorts make my ass look fatter?" I asked with my eyes glued to the floor-length mirror inside the designer clothing store.

I could tell Sweatt put it on her ass something serious last night, because the "somewhere" we had to be was shopping and she made it clear she was buying, so you know I had to make it count. What bitch didn't like a free shopping spree?

"Yeah, they do a little bit," she responded, staring at me from the back. "But I bet you can't even make your ass clap, that's how

I know you got a big ass for nothing." I turned to face her and smiled, because I could feel all the hate coming from her.

"Is that a challenge?" I asked.

"If that's how you wanna take it, but time is ticking and that ass ain't clapping yet." I walked into the dressing room to undress as I heard the soft sound of Beyoncé's voice playing throughout the store. *How the hell was I going to dance to that*? I thought. Champagne wouldn't give a damn, long as she could make me look bad, she was alright.

So, I said, "Fuck it," and sashayed out the dressing room wearing only my bra and panties. I grinned at Champagne and proceeded to the mirror as I dropped down and got my eagle on, making my ass clap like two hands.

"Clap! Clap! Clap! Clap!" I repeated, looking back at it. I was loving the feeling of just getting loose and wild, because I had never acted or exposed myself in public before. The next thing I knew, Beyoncé was replaced by Rihanna and the hit single, "Work" flowed through the P.A. system as I dropped down into a split, while I continued to make my ass clap one cheek at a time.

"Oh, hell naw!" Champagne shouted as she dropped her Robin's Jeans to the floor and stepped out of them, before tossing her shirt over her head. She stood right next to me in her pink boy shorts and bra, twerking like she was in a throwback Uncle Luke music video. A crowd had begun to form after one gentleman stopped working to watch us like he was a teenager just hitting puberty.

"Damn, I'm glad I came to this store," somebody else in the crowd shouted. We smiled at each other and began making our asses clap even faster, loving the attention we were receiving from so many strangers.

"What the hell kind of freak shit y'all doing over here? My grandkids are in here," an older woman yelled, breaking up the show. That was our cue to get the hell out of there, so fast as we could, we slipped back into our clothes and hauled ass out of there with our arms full of expensive designer shit for the five-finger discount the ghetto way. Once leaving the clothing store, we ended up right next door in an adult sex shop browsing around to see all the kinky shit they had to offer.

"Champagne, look at this shit, there have to be some freaky ass bitches out there in the world to buy this shit," I said excitedly, grabbing a pair of crotchless panties and nipple clippers.

"That's nothing, look at this big ass dick. I'll suck the skin off this thing," Champagne responded, showing me the ten-inch dildo, before sliding it in her mouth and demonstrating her golden head skills. I looked at her in surprise and burst into laughter because not only did she have the dildo in her mouth without paying for it, she was also slapping herself in the face with it and all, while moaning and making facial expressions like it was the real thing.

"Girl, you done gone crazy, puttin your mouth on these people shit," I said, trying to take the dildo while looking around to see if anybody was watching us. "Besides, this thing is too big for you anyway, you wouldn't know what to do with it." She stopped, then looked at me like I had a big ass booger in my nose, with her head tilted to the side and her hands on her hips.

"You telling me you know what to do with it, Ms. Super Head?"

"You damn right! I bet I can deep throat the whole thing without choking or gagging," I stated confidently. She stared at me once again before sucking her teeth, indicating that she didn't believe me. Soon as I saw the smirk on her face, I grabbed the dildo and brought it towards my mouth to start sucking. With my mouth wide and both hands around the base, I started from the bottom and licked my way all the way up to the head, soaking it with my saliva before letting it ease into my mouth and down my throat.

I kept my eyes on her, so I could once again see the hate while I performed. We were so deep into my performance, we both forgot we weren't alone and inside a public place where anybody could see me.

"Ma'am! Ma'am, you are not allowed to test the product before you buy it," the overweight, freckle-faced white man at the cash register shouted, before walking up behind us. He surprised us both with his presence and it was at that moment I gagged and dropped the dildo.

"I told you! I knew you couldn't do it!" Champagne shouted excitedly, while jumping up and down. I shot the white man a unit so hard if looks could kill, he would've been dead as that dildo on the floor.

"Ma'am, I'm going to have to ask you two to—"

"Naw, bitch! That shit don't even count. That cracka scared the shit out of me," I shouted, cutting the white man off and ignoring his attempt to say anything. After another attempt, he raised his voice a little, which caused the both of us to stare at each other before going in on his ass with a rant session.

"Cracka, who you think you talking to? Over there looking like a fat-ass child molester," Champagne said, laughing at her own joke.

"Fa'real, looking like an overweight Harry Potter with the thick ass glasses," I joined in by laughing with her. He was getting so angry from the embarrassment we were causing him, his face turned red as a hot chili pepper and he exploded like a volcano, lashing out at us.

"You two have disrespected me for the last time, so there's no more Mr. Nice Guy. Get the hell out of my store now!" We both looked at each other in silence before laughing uncontrollably as we headed towards the door.

"I saw that little Vienna sausage of yours get hard when you were watching me suck that dildo, you fat-ass pervert," I blurted out one last time as we both continued to laugh, before walking out the store with my phone ringing out of control. I ignored it though, because Champagne and I still had unfinished business to tend to. The bitch thought she was better than me in everything, so I was about to show her ass that she wasn't, period.

Chapter 16

E'mani

I still was kind of shocked at how little I knew about my supposed-to-be sister, Mahogany. I mean, that bitch was a fuckin mass murderer. I never knew she had that many bodies under her belt and the shit scared me, but I knew I had to grow some balls and get my mind right. A couple weeks had passed since the last time Mahogany or Agent Watson visited me in the hospital, and I haven't heard from either of them since. I couldn't believe the bitch wanted me to set Mahogany up or she was gone hide my ass under the prison, but I told her I would, just to buy myself enough time to come up with my own plan.

I was due to be released today, not all the way healed, but at least I was able to use the bathroom like normal people. Once my release papers were signed, my mother was ready to take me home and when I say home, I mean her home. I didn't have any plans of staying there long, so it really didn't matter to me as I lay in my old bed and stared at the ceiling.

My thoughts quickly shifted to Dontay, the fine ass C.O. I met in the county jail. I had caught myself daydreaming about him on many occasions while in the hospital and I really wanted to know how he was doing, but at the same time it's been a while since I had a chance to speak to him, and I was definitely afraid of rejection.

Should I call him now or should I wait? I thought as I continued staring at the ceiling with my cell phone stuck to my ear as if I was talking to somebody. I had been doing this for the last ten minutes, debating on whether I should call. I was starting to get mad at my damn self because I knew I was acting like a young schoolgirl. After a while I finally made up my mind, took a deep breath and dialed the number, praying he answered. Four rings later, I was listening to his voicemail. I wasn't the type of female to leave messages on a nigga phone I didn't really know, to me it was a sign you were desperate, and that wasn't me. I hung up then called right back, really not expecting him to answer, just calling so I could say I called twice. The third ring he answered, and it really caught my ass by surprise.

"Yoo, who dis?" he asked. More nervous than a rabbit inside of a snake hole, I built up the courage and stated my name in the most sexiest voice I could muster, praying he didn't forget who I was and making me look like a stalker. "E'mani?" Dontay repeated to himself, but loud enough to where I could still hear him. After about thirty seconds of thinking about it, I guess he finally remembered, and it showed from the excitement in his voice.

"Damn! How's it going? I was wondering when you were going to call me, I been waiting on this call."

"Oh, really? It doesn't seem that way to me. You didn't even know who I was" I responded. I didn't know if Dontay really was waiting on my call or what. I do know I was just as eager to call, but the thought of being rejected fully took control of my mind.

"Naw, it ain't like that. I just don't answer numbers I don't know and besides, I haven't heard from you in weeks. What's up with that?" Now I could give him the real rundown of what happened with me and my girls, or I could just give a bullshit ass story until I knew more about him, but at the same time I had to tell him something. I thought about this for a couple seconds, before I started questioning myself about why I would lie to a nigga I didn't even know like that.

"I was in the hospital, recovering from being shot. The same day I was released from jail, I ended up getting shot at my welcome home celebration, ain't that's some shit?" I said, still feeling kind of shy.

"Damn, shawty, fa'real? I heard about somebody getting killed at a night club the day you got out, but I had no idea you got hit too. I hope you a'ight, shawty, because you're too fine to be gettin shot. I'm also glad you called. I thought you stood a nigga up because knowing you, I know you got too many niggas on your team," he responded. I opened my mouth in shock, forming a perfect circle. I couldn't believe what he just said, is he serious?

"Boy! I know you just didn't go there. All them C.O. hoes you got running behind you. I heard them bitches talking about how you fucked them, especially that bitch officer Davis," I said, rolling over on my stomach after placing a pillow under me. "They also talked about how good you were with your tongue." Dontay took the phone away from his mouth before covering it with his hand, but I could still hear him laughing on the other end. From what I've heard, I know Dontay knew females loved getting their pussy ate and unlike a lot of black men, he wasn't afraid to use his tongue. So, soon as I heard him get back on the phone, I asked the one question I had been dying to know since we first met.

"On a scale from one to ten and ten being the highest, how good can you eat pussy?"

"Damn, shawty, so we throwing questions like that at each other now?" he quickly replied, still laughing for some odd reason, but I was dead ass serious.

"Don't answer my question with a question, that's very rude," I said, catching myself smiling. "I wanna know how good you are, because if you good as people say, then I hit the jackpot and caught me a certified golden head." We both laughed, barely able to control ourselves and almost forgetting we were on the phone.

"You're crazy and very outspoken. I like it though, I can't lie. But on a scale from one to ten, I'll have to say get another scale, because ten ain't high enough. When the time comes where I can really show you how I put it down, I'll let you be the judge of it. I'm just that confident," he said, making me wetter by the second. I was loving the way Dontay talked with his thuggish swag. We went into every subject I could think of, turning our "getting to know each other" phone call into a three-hour, sex hot line.

It was two o'clock in the morning when we got off the phone, and I was so excited about spending time with him later today that I was nowhere near sleepy. I thought about touching myself and putting out the fire he started between my legs, but that thought quickly vanished when the image of my mother busting into my room and catching me with my hand deep in my pussy popped into my head. I smiled before playing some Alicia Keys, then continued to stare at the ceiling until I fell asleep.

Dontay showed up about noon and took me to Applebee's for our first date. I was nervous as hell feeling the butterflies flying around in my stomach, because believe it or not, this was actually the first real date I have ever been on. Most of my previous boy-friends just brought me things and thought it would make up for the time we didn't spend together, but I could tell Dontay was old-fashioned.

We walked in, ordered drinks and chit chatted while we looked over the menu. I kept stealing glances at Dontay, admiring every-thing about him. He really cleaned up nice and looked handsome outside of his work uniform. *I could really see myself having a fu-ture with him, I'm talking kids and all*, I thought as I hid my face behind my menu and smiled to myself. I was so caught up in myself, I still had no clue of what I wanted when the waitress showed up with our drinks. I was so embarrassed, and I guess it showed all over my face because Dontay stepped in and ordered us both a well-done peppered steak, and potatoes with a salad on the side. I thanked him right before he stared me in the eyes, causing me to feel a little un-comfortable.

"What! I have something on my face or something? Please don't tell me I have a booger in my nose," I said, panicking while grabbing my purse in search of a mirror. I could tell I really tickled him because he was just laughing out of control, but if you ask me, I didn't think it wasn't really that damn funny.

"I'm sorry, baby. I didn't mean to laugh at you, but I was just thinking about how you look so much more beautiful without the jail house jumpsuit," he said, sounding so serious, but that really didn't make the fact that he was laughing at me any better. The food arrived a short time later and after about an hour of enjoying myself, I didn't want to end it so soon but not being one to question my man, I followed right behind him to the car. We rode in silence for the most part other than the music, but out of the blue I started feeling horny and thinking how it would feel to have him inside me for the first time.

We walked into his house and I swear, it was nothing like the place of a bachelor, it felt more like a home than a house as everything was luxurious, from the window curtains to the marbled floors. I moaned softly and closed my eyes as Dontay grabbed me from behind and slowly started undressing me once my feet touched the plush carpet in the living room. Part of me wanted this so badly, but the other half kept telling me I was moving too fast.

I was so confused, mainly because Dontay was very slow and ever so gentle with me. It took him nearly thirty minutes to slide down my panties to expose the landing strip of hair at the apex of my thighs and the large purplish labia guarding the entrance of my pussy. After I was completely naked, he undressed himself before guiding me to the bedroom, where he laid me down on the bed and mounted me. I immediately clenched up as he placed what seemed like the biggest penis I had ever felt at the entrance of my pussy. It was like my pussy just closed up tight and he was unable to enter me.

After feeling his kisses, I relaxed my body then climbed on top of him to place my pussy in his face. I guess I wasn't ready to have him inside me just yet. He spread my legs slightly apart and the light pressure of his fingers were just enough to part my pouting lip exposing the light purplish pink of my pussy like an open rose. There was no doubting my arousal as my erect clit peeped out of its sheltering hood. Dontay drove his tongue deep inside me as he sucked my labia tenderly, then sucked on my swollen clit. Lifting my ass cheeks, he eased me toward him, now about to lick all the way up and down my slit.

"Mmmm… baby, that feels so good," I moaned softly. I closed my eyes again and threw my head back, whimpering loudly as my pleasure grew. My clit hardened even more and my pussy tightened around his tongue. Then I let out a high-pitched moan, grinding my hips and pulling his head as I came. Once Dontay sucked my pussy clean, I bent over the bed in the doggie style position, with him standing behind me.

"Oh, God!" I moaned as my labia opened up, accepting his dick the second time. "I want you to fuck me hard, baby, don't worry about being gentle." As his hands rested on my hips, I could feel his dick thrusting deep inside me as I pushed back against him, moaning how good he felt.

"You want all this dick, baby? Ha? Let me know," he asked. I couldn't help it, just the sound of his voice was making me wetter and that's all it took.

"Oh... oh yes, baby. I want it all, please fuck me harder," I groaned, shaking as I was having my second orgasm of the night. Once I caught my breath, I had him lie down on his back, then I crawled up his body, positioning my dripping wet pussy over his still hard dick and slowly lowered myself onto it until he was in me all the way. I started to fuck him using just my pussy muscles. As I gripped his dick, he began to slide his hands across my ass. The sensation of having my pussy grip his dick while the rest of my body stayed still was hard to describe.

Neither of us had ever felt anything like it before, it was just something I wanted to try that came to my mind in the middle of our love making. After thirty seconds of him caressing my ass while I squeezed his dick, we both came together in what had to be the most intense orgasm I had ever had.

We lay together enjoying the afterglow of the amazing sex we just had as I played with the hair on his chest. It had been awhile since a man made me feel this good and I never wanted the feeling to go away. I told Dontay about the situation I was in but left out the part of me having any involvement. I explained that a federal agent wanted me to snitch and help her take down the closest friend I've ever had. He claimed he felt where I was coming from and his advice was that I shouldn't cooperate, but what choice did I really have?

"I don't mean no disrespect, so please don't feel offended. But I heard through the grapevine that your home girl was as backstabbing as they come, so why would you want to help her anyway?" Dontay asked, watching me as I listened to his heartbeat. I didn't feel offended at all, because I know a lot of people didn't like Mahogany or the Baller Babies and would say anything to tarnish their names. But they were my girls and I felt the need to speak up for them in their absence.

"I don't take it as disrespect but to clear the smoke, all the grapevine gossipers as you say, don't know Mahogany. Yeah, she can be ruthless, shit... we all can and you can take this to the bank and cash it. Mahogany will stab you in your chest before she stabs you in your back and I've witnessed that." We both lay there quiet for about twenty minutes. I could tell he was really thinking about what I said and realizing how much love I had for Mahogany. Damn, I wish I really knew what was going on inside his head.

"Listen, E'mani," he started. "I don't want you involved in no bullshit, but I can tell by the way you talk about Mahogany that you gone do whatever you can to help her, no matter what. So, against my better judgement, I'll help you with a little something." I smiled, thinking he cared about me enough to involve himself in something illegal, even if it was just him doing something small for me. He then asked if I've ever shot a gun and the first thought that popped in my head was Neeko and the way I blew off half of his face, but I kept that thought and told Dontay a bold-faced lie.

"No, I've never shot a gun before. I mean, I've held one, but I didn't fire it," I answered. At that moment, he jumped up and scrambled to find his clothes, while telling me to get dressed and go to the car. I was confused because we just had sex, so I would've preferred to take a shower before I left the house, but that wasn't an option. In the car, he explained where we were going and decided on telling me the story of how they met, he didn't care if I wanted to hear it or not, which I didn't, but I didn't have a choice.

"It was about two years ago that I found this private gun range owned by this retired military captain by the name of Tank. Tank was at least six-four and about two hundred and thirty pounds of muscles, he was a big dude. I guess I caught his attention by the way I was shooting, which was like somebody gave Ray Charles a gun. But hey, that's what I was there for, to learn. He stepped to me with a friendly conversation, but being young and dumb, I acted tough and never said a word back.

'Listen, little homie, you're shooting like shit. When you're trying to hit your target, aim your pistol just below it so when you pull the trigger, the pressure from the bullet being forced out won't cause the gun to jerk upwards so high,' he said. I was still playing tough but couldn't help peeping over my shoulders to see if he was watching as I followed his advice.

"The next couple rounds went smooth and I started to loosen up, finally giving in. We talked for what seemed like hours and Tank had my full attention. First asking if I was the police, which he told me later that he was just joking, then he used to collect guns and was now trying to get rid of many as he could. After telling some girl to take over and help people who were still shooting, he took me to the back of the gun range, where we came to a stainless-steel door, the size of a Sub-Zero refrigerator. My eyes were so wide that I didn't dare blink, thinking I would miss something once I saw the room full of guns and then the rest of his history."

I swear, the whole time he was talking, all I remember hearing is something about a room full of guns behind the gun range. I hope he never tells me that long and boring ass story again, because I'll literally go fucking crazy.

Once he finished his story, it wasn't thirty minutes later before we pulled in front of a beautiful white house, which I'm guessing belonged to Tank. Now, I've seen some beautiful houses before, but this one took breathtaking to a whole other level. We got out the car and walked towards the front door but as we did, I could hear sounds of soft moans coming from somewhere close.

"Hold up!" I said, stopping and trying to make sure I wasn't losing my mind. Dontay looked at me with a stale face, letting me know he was confused.

"What's going on? You alright?" he asked, but all I could do was tell him to listen, and then we both heard it. They were definitely moans of pleasure and couldn't be mistaken for anything else. We looked at each other and couldn't help but smile, thinking we had just finished doing the exact same thing a couple hours ago. Once we finally made it to the front door and knocked, Tank showed up in his robe with two white girls on each side of him.

Now, it was safe to say Tank was a handsome man and I wouldn't mind giving up the kitty to him, but he just as quickly turned me off when I saw them two white bitches. I wouldn't say that I was a hater, well I take that back because I lied. I hated to see our black man with these white bitches even though I'm Filipino and Jamaican, I'm still considered black.

"What's going on, lil homie?" Tank asked Dontay, but at the same time brought me back to realty as he looked like a proud pimp showing off his two white money makers.

"I see we caught you at a bad time. We didn't mean to interrupt, maybe we should come back at a different time," Dontay replied. I looked at him as if his head was shrinking right in front of my eyes, because he had to be crazy to think I was taking this ride with him again. But luckily, Tank saw it in my demeanor and said the right thing.

"Naw! That's crazy. You don't have to go anywhere, every-thing's cool. Right, ladies?" Tank said, more so talking to the white bitches as they answered in unison, almost making me want to throw up right in their faces. After a little more small talk, Tank invited us in to talk about the reason we drove all the way out of the city limits to visit him. He sat across from Dontay and me, cigar in his mouth with the confidence of a man who had just won millions of dollars.

"What do I owe the pleasure of seeing you again, lil homie? Because I know it's about business, or you wouldn't have drove all this way out here," Tank asked, but eyed me like I looked good enough to eat. I bet it had everything to do with him smelling the scent of my freshly fucked kitty in the air, because even though two hours passed since Dontay was inside of me, I was still soaking wet.

"Tank, my girl and I came to see if you had time to give her a couple lessons in the gun range and we also needed to get our hands on some burners." Silence took over the room for about two minutes before Tank sent the two white girls out, while telling me to follow. I didn't know what the hell he had going on, so I didn't move until Dontay told me it was okay. Despite how I first felt about the white girls, they actually turned out to be cool and within an hour had me on the verge of becoming a vet on using automatic handguns.

After a while I was starting to wonder where Dontay went off to, so I went searching like the typical suspicious black girl, until I came up on a vault-looking door. The first thing that came to my mind was the gun room Dontay told me about, so without further thought, I let myself in and really couldn't believe what I was actually seeing.

Chapter 17

Mahogany

"All this time, this nigga was fuckin playing me," I shouted the second Champagne answered her phone, not giving her a chance to say anything. "I can't believe I fell for all that bullshit again. After everything Supreme took me through and after all the pep talks, I gave myself about never trusting a man again. He gotta go, Champagne. I can't let this shit ride, so I need y'all back in St. Pete today." I was so fucking fired up that I hung up the phone without saying bye. I really needed to get my mind right, because I was taught not to make permanent decisions off temporary emotions, they always seem to come back to bite you in the ass. That lesson came from experience.

Time passed and I came up with a quick plan I was pretty sure would end his career, but in case it didn't, we had to find somewhere else to live, because I'm one hundred percent sure it was going to be the beginning of a war. On the other hand, I still needed to get in contact with E'mani to let her know what was going on, but knowing her mother was probably still at the hospital with her, I wouldn't dare show my face up there again.

I try to hold my tongue much as I could around Mrs. Newman because she was E'mani's mother, but I knew the old bitch didn't like me. Shit, everybody knew she blamed me as the cause of E'mani's troubled life. I called the hospital instead, planning on leaving a message, but was told E'mani had been discharged two days ago.

"What the hell!" I thought out loud, now feeling confused about why E'mani hadn't called to inform me that her Shrek-looking ass was out the hospital. I was definitely feeling some type of way and wasted no time calling her line.

"Bitch, where you at?" I asked soon as I heard her greet me in her white girl voice. She laughed like she already knew I would be calling and going off on her ass.

"No bitch, where you at?" she shot back playing games but sounding like a little girl who didn't know how to use curse words but tried.

"Listen E'mani, I don't play games and neither do I have time for them, you out of all people should know that. It's some serious shit I have to tell you, but I'm not saying shit over this phone, so I need you to come home like right now." I could tell she caught on quickly that I meant what I said and probably less than two minutes later, she was walking through the front door. I mean, it was so sudden I still had my phone to my ear yelling her name, telling her to answer me.

"You were outside the whole fuckin time?" I asked, feeling like a donkey's ass before taking the phone away from my ear.

"Does it matter? You said you needed me home like right now, well here I am," she shot back. E"mani was really starting to get beside herself and I was a second away from illustrating on her ass, but I wanted Rue more, so I swallowed my pride. That's something I never do and then I told her the whole story about what happened between me and Rue, and why I needed her to call the realtor so we could move.

"Well, Rue is the least of your worries," she started, before challenging me in a stare down. "The FBI is trying to bring a federal indictment against you, and they tried to get me to help them. A bitch named Agent Watson came to visit me in the hospital and guess what she had with her? Pictures of all the bodies you got under your belt: Supreme, Doe Boy, your cousin Shay, Ja'mya and Kayla. You really been busy. I'm supposed to be your sister and you never told me about Doe Boy, your cousin Shay or that you had something to do with Supreme getting killed."

Who the hell this bitch think she is? I don't have to tell her a damn thing if I don't want to. That's my fuckin business not hers. Now, she done got me started.

"Okay, since you want to go there, you never told me that you also had something to do with Supreme's death. Yeah, you sent a hit on his ass too. I know all about that." We were now going back and forth with each other, yelling at the top of our lungs.

I stepped closer to get rid of the space between me and her, and it surprised the hell out of me when she didn't back down. She stood her ground, ready to go toe-to-toe with me if it went that far. Jail had really changed her. I didn't want to hurt E'mani, but her boldness was about to really push me over the edge, so it was a good thing Champagne and Passion walked in when they did.

"What the hell going on?" Champagne asked, stepping between us trying to defuse the situation. Neither of us said a word as Champagne and Passion watched E'mani and I continue our stare down. I knew what she wanted, and I wasn't going to be the one to back down, so we could either find out the hard way or the easy way, it didn't matter to me.

"I guess loyalty really ain't promised, but to show you how real I am, I'm still going all in with you against Rue and anybody else on your shit list," E'mani stated, before walking off. While she went to do whatever she was going to do, I took that time to give Champagne and Passion the 411 on what was going on. I told them everything about me and Rue that I couldn't say over the phone and even the shit E'mani told me about the FBI.

I didn't really want to confide in anybody but that shit with the feds was scaring the hell out of me. I mean, how did they know I was the one that killed Doe Boy, Shay, Ja'mya or even Kayla? I made sure to cover my tracks and not leave any evidence. Then Shanel popped into my head. Could that bitch have been working as a CI? It really wouldn't surprise me after all the shit I found in her room. I glanced at Champagne and Passion as I came back to reality, because I knew I looked like I was losing my mind as I stared off in space while mumbling.

E'mani returned to the living room, now carrying a Gucci duffle bag and in better spirits. I guess she wasn't letting the little disagreement we had get to her. "Here's the news. I just got off the phone with my realtor and she said she could sell the house in a couple months. But, on the other hand, how do East Tampa sound as our new residence?" she said as she sat the bag next to her feet.

We all looked at each other trying to read the other's expression to see what they thought about everything. I didn't really care where

I lived because I was one of them bitches that could adapt to any projects. Champagne and Passion both stated they didn't mind, even though they were further away from their hometown of Gainesville, and E'mani liked the idea more than any of us, because she says it will get her further away from her mother. I knew that feeling of wanting to get away from somebody, but at the end of the day, her mother loved her and just wanted to make sure she was alright.

I pointed towards the bag, indicating I wanted to know what was in it and E'mani gave a look as if she forgot it was even there, before smiling and then unzipping it. One at a time, she pulled out at least ten guns, ranging from small .22 Rugers to big .357 Magnums with the serial numbers scratched off every last one of them. "Bitch, where the hell you get all these damn guns from?" I asked excitedly but surprised all at the same time, while Champagne and Passion both wasted no time grabbing their favorite ones as if they would somehow disappear right in front of their eyes. E'mani continued to smile like a proud mother watching her children on Christmas morning before she spoke.

"Do you remember what I told you the day we ran down on Ja'mya and you asked me about the two guns I had? Well, ain't nothing changed, the plug still fuck with a bitch." Out of all people in the world, I never thought it would be E'mani who would come through for a bitch. I low-key wanted to hug and kiss her on the cheeks like the Italians did when they greeted each other, but I didn't need her thinking I was on that bisexual shit like she did the day we danced at Magic City for Doe Boy's birthday and we ended up locking lips.

"Listen, this the deal," I started after getting everybody's attention. "E'mani, go ahead and finalize everything with the move to East Tampa, because I want us to start packing and get out of here soon as possible. Once that's taken care of, we gone throw Rue a party like he never had before. It's literally gone be to die for, so we gotta come correct." We all went our separate ways and out of nowhere, I started feeling nauseous as I walked to my room. I held onto the wall to keep myself from tumbling over and then ran right past my room and into the bathroom, barely making it to the commode before vomiting everywhere.

"What the hell is wrong with me?" I asked myself, more so thinking out loud. I wiped the saliva from around my mouth before looking around to make sure nobody could see me on my knees hugging the toilet, but it was too late. E'mani, followed by Champagne and Passion, came running towards the bathroom as if they were missing a show.

"Bitch, we heard somebody throwing up, so we came running. What, you sucked some bad dick and it's now catching up with your nasty ass?" Champagne joked, getting a laugh out of everybody. I played it off and laughed too, but that shit she said low-key made me feel some type of way. Once I finally got off the floor, I explained that I was just sick with a head cold and stomachache before gargling water in my mouth to get rid of the foul aftertaste.

"Naw, bitch, that ain't no damn cold. I know them symptoms, your whore-ish ass pregnant," Champagne said, again putting her two cents in like I really wanted to hear that shit. I shook my head no because I knew I wasn't pregnant. I couldn't get pregnant, and that came out the doctor's mouth when I was fifteen and had my fourth miscarriage.

"Look, y'all need to go finish packing, or whatever the hell you was doing and get out my business, like now!" I demanded, getting sick of them always saying something negative and killing a bitch's joy with the bullshit. They all left the bathroom laughing, as Champagne and now Passion continued to crack jokes on me about being pregnant. I headed to my room to start something I dreaded doing and that was packing. Well, I was just gone pack the most important things myself and the rest was getting moved by the moving truck company I'm about to hire.

E'mani, Champagne, Passion and I all drove behind the moving truck in separate cars to our new spot in East Tampa. All of a sudden, I felt kinda of excited to be starting fresh in a new location where nobody knew us. At first, the move was only because I didn't want to be around if Rue's people found out anything when I played my trump card. But now, I looked forward to starting over. And plus, I always wanted to visit the Hard Rock Hotel and Casino.

Surprisingly, the new house was posher than the last one and located in a good neighborhood. Harbor Island to be exact, so we didn't have to worry about any bullshit. Then, to make things more interesting, we found out Champagne's favorite rapper Plies lived about four houses down, so you know that bitch was going crazy. She was even starting to act like a damn stalker the way she jogged past the man's house every five minutes to try and catch him when he came outside. E'mani and I were still bumping heads and this time, it was over who would get the master bedroom, which I damn sure wasn't about to let her get.

"Illustrate on who? Bitch, you better get yo mind right before I beat your ass in here. E'mani, don't fuckin play with me, you musta forgot I stay on safe mode," I stated bluntly, tryna get it through her thick skull that I was serious as a heart attack. I don't know what all she went through behind them gates, but jail really had changed her, and she needed to know I wasn't the fucking enemy.

"Listen, Mahogany, we're not getting anywhere going back and forth with each other like this. I mean, we're both grown ass women. Why the hell we're always arguing about the simplest shit? You can have the master bedroom," she said, before walking off like she was doing me a damn favor. I laughed to keep myself from saying anything else, because one thing I don't do is chase after a bitch and beg for their forgiveness. I went and got myself a glass of water before finding a spot on the floor, because I was starting to feel lightheaded again. Honestly, I think it was the fact that my blood pressure was high, and I was under a lot of stress. That alone I knew would cause complications to your body.

"Girl, you alright?" I heard a voice ask before I actually saw the face, but when I did look up, Passion was staring me in the face as if she was trying to look into my soul. The worried look she displayed was obvious and I really didn't need her or anybody else bringing the fact that I might be pregnant back up, so I simply told her a lie and didn't feel bad about doing so.

"I'm alright, I'm just a little exhausted from all this packing, moving and then unpacking again. I think I need to go lay down and take me a quick nap and hopefully, the moving company will have everything unpacked when I wake up."

It was about two hours later when E'mani came waking me up with my ringing cell phone in her hand. I shot her one of my "bitch, you got to be crazy" looks, mad that she woke me up out of a good fuckin dream, and then snatched my phone away from her as she walked off laughing. Damn, she was starting to get on my last nerve. I answered the phone without looking at the screen but knew exactly who it was once I heard the familiar voice.

"I'm not going to hang up. I'm actually glad you called. Rue, I want to apologize for the way I overreacted. At the time it was just a lot for me to take in and I didn't know how to handle it. But I been doing some serious soul searching and I honestly don't want to lose you, so I'm willing to give it a try. But, if I'm gone play my position, then you better make sure them bitches play theirs," I said, confessing to him how I felt before giving him a chance to say what he had to say. It turned out that he was more afraid of losing me than anything and wanted me to come over so he could make it up to me.

"I'll come over only if I can make it up to you instead. I have a couple friends and we wanna throw you a surprise party," I said, before we hung up. Now, I know it might sound crazy with all the shit I just confessed, but it's more than one way to skin a cat and if you've ever seen the movie *State Property 2,* then you know exactly what I mean when I say "surprise party."

Once I got off the phone, my first destination was the kitchen. The aroma of the spicy dishes had my stomach doing summersaults as it growled. It was nothing new to have the house smelling like a soul food joint, but the way E'mani mixed things together, she really put her foot in it this time. Thanks to Passion, we all sat at the dining room table and ate as a family. I was really surprised there was no arguing going on, even though at times I knew somebody wanted to say something.

At first, it was kind of somber, but we slowly worked our way into a simple conversation, before I told them about the phone call with Rue. I needed all them to be on their A-game because we had no time for mistakes. Like the Baller Babies are known for doing, we had to make this party rememberable.

E'mani ended up having a small heart-to-heart with everybody at the table, well, mainly me. She apologized for anything she may have done to offend any of us, and to me for not being the friend I needed her to be. She said she didn't want to fight against me anymore and rather with me. I can't lie, she had me on the verge of tears, but I held them back because my pride was too big and I didn't want to seem like I was a weak bitch in front of them. Maybe one day I'll learn to express my feelings to somebody other than the person I'm fucking, but until then, I gotta keep my repetition as that bitch.

"Look… E'mani, you're my sister no matter what. But you've done enough by providing us with the things we need the most, and that's protection. You really don't have to go to the party, you can sit this one out if you want to," I said, not knowing if she was really ready for what she was getting into, because there was no turning back. To my surprise, she declined my suggestion with the shake of her head before speaking, and that made me feel like a proud captain, knowing one of my soldiers would rather be on the front line with me.

"It's about that time I put in some more work and besides, I can't let y'all have all the fun. And Mahogany, don't ever insult me like that again. It's always Double B's, bitch!"

With that being said, we all started screaming, "Double B's" as if we were auditioning to become hype men. The rest of the day was like a family reunion, because we hung out and had fun as if we hadn't seen each other in years. The Baller Babies were back, and I can't explain how good it felt. I just hope it don't be so many secrets this time around.

I went to sleep that night, wondering how the rest of my life would turn out. I mean, there's no way of knowing what would happen at Rue's surprise party tomorrow. I still don't know if I would like the rest of my days spent in a federal penitentiary, being that I have some bitch named Agent Watson tryna catch me for a body.

Then, on top of that, I still low-key don't trust the bitches in my circle. "God, please protect me," was the last thing I said before closing my eyes that night.

"I'm on my way now, baby, you gone love the surprise I have for you," I said to Rue as E'mani, Champagne, Passion and I all jumped in the car with one thing on our minds. We were all dressed in lingerie, covered by black trench coats and white stilettos to complement our sexy attire. No matter how many times I've been down this road, I still felt nervous at this time. E'mani who gave me the advice I needed to do what I came to do, and that was to give Rue the surprise party of a lifetime, the Double B way!

We drove through the gates and came up to familiar faces. All four of us opened our coats, giving out samples of what the rest of the night may have in store for them, before telling everybody to head to the back, which we claimed were orders from Rue. Once reaching our destination, we all jumped out the car, first making sure we were on safe mode and then sashayed into the building like we owned that muthafucka.

Keith Williams

Chapter 18

Champagne

Upon entering the double doors that led into the building, Passion, Mahogany, E'mani and I all became the center of attention as we strutted across the marble floor, looking like thicker versions of Victoria's Secret models once we dropped our coats. I was so ready for some action I could feel myself getting moist, just from thinking about what was next to come. I guess Mahogany felt the same because she wasted no time walking up to Rue before letting him sample her fingers, after swiping them between her pussy lips. I wasn't a lesbian or anything like that but damn, my girl looked sexy the way she took control over the whole party like a boss bitch, and I could tell every man in this bitch agreed by the way they cheered and probably wished they could trade places with Rue at this very moment.

She then grabbed Rue's hands, placed them on her ass and led him into the privacy of the back room silently passing the floor to me as I reached into my bag and took out bottles of Cîroc and Dom P. I was feeling a little extra, so I popped everybody off with a half-gram of Molly just to set the mood right and as the drugs started to take effect, I seductively grabbed Passion and E'mani to give the men a show as we swung our hips and slow danced to the song, "12 Play." R. Kelly really made the mood perfect with his intoxicating voice and as E'mani and Passion got into the groove of things, we never missed a beat as we followed his every command.

"Four... lie down on the floor, Five... I cannot wait to come inside..." Every man in here looked as if he was ready to stick his dick in any moist hole he could find, no matter who it belonged to and my girls took advantage as we blindfolded them, before stripping them naked and teasing their hard-on's. The sounds they made when they thought only we could hear them was hilarious to say the least, but like the saying goes, all good things have to come to an end and that was the truth.

Now, for the final act of the night, we took turns pouring bottles of Dom P into their open mouths, but by the time the bottles were half-empty, their bodies begun to jerk uncontrollably as white foam clogged their esophagi. Yes, we poisoned their ass by spiking the liquor with hydrogen cyanide, before sending a single bullet to every last head, killing them muthafuckas like the plan-B, morning-after pill. Dat part!

We all stood back and admired our work of art as we waited on Mahogany to complete her part of the mission, and just as we started to get impatient, we caught sight of Rue's naked body running out the side door as Mahogany sent multiple bullets his way, missing every shot.

"What the fuck!" I shouted to Mahogany, wanting to know what went wrong on her end, but all I got was the silent treatment as she went around the apartment wiping down everything we may have touched. I continued shooting questions at her, not liking the fact I was being ignored, but I guess I struck the wrong nerve because she lashed out like I've never seen before.

"What the fuck you want me to say, Champagne? Huh? Do you see all these dead bodies? Unless you want to go to prison for the rest of your life, get your shit together and let's go!" There was nothing else to be said as I followed the orders that were given to me because she was right, and I hate that it took her blowing up in my face in front of E'mani and Passion to get my mind right. It had to be that damn Molly in my system but trust me, that was the last fucking time.

Once we had all of our stuff together, we made Molotov cocktails with the remaining bottles of alcohol and tossed them across the room before hauling ass to the car and driving all the way back to East Tampa. I still wanted to know how the hell Mahogany managed to let Rue get away. I mean, he was the whole reason for us taking this field trip and now we all have to be extra cautious, because slippers do count.

I kept my mouth closed like everybody else and enjoyed the mellow sound of Ella Mai's voice as we approached the interstate. It was in the wee hours of the morning when we made it home and

I couldn't begin to explain how happy I was to get in my bed and go to sleep.

"Champagne! Guess what this bitch had the nerve to ask me?" I heard Passion scream as she tried to beat down my bedroom door. I glanced at the alarm clock on the side of my bed before silently curing her ass out and then playing sleep once I read it said, 8:45. *I'll be damn if I get out my bed just to entertain her bullshit*, I thought as the door swung open.

"Bitch, what the fuck you want?" I shouted, pulling the comforter over my naked body as she caught me off guard.

"What the fuck ever, I've seen that raggedy ass pussy a million times, so I don't know why you tryna cover up," she shot back causing me to burst into laughter, so I know she smell my morning breath. Even though I was laughing that's one thing I did not like, a bitch all in my face when I haven't even brushed my teeth or washed my ass. I knew she wasn't going anywhere until she said what she had to say, so I gave her my attention, trying to make this conversation quick as possible.

"Do you remember that stank pussy ass hoe who called my phone the other day, talking about she found my number in her man's pocket?" Passion questioned. I shook my head yeah, even though I had no clue of what the hell she was talking about. But that was easier than me saying I didn't remember, and she start telling me about the first story all over again.

"Well, she just called again and had the nerve to ask me if her man was with me, because he didn't come home last night, and his kids miss him. "

"No, the hell she didn't!" I blurted out, not believing she was actually telling me the truth.

"Yeah, that bitch did, and you know what I told her? If she took care of herself right and cleaned that stank ass pussy, maybe he'll come home at night. A man doesn't want to smell fish all the time," Passion said, looking like she was about to have a flashback. I laughed and laughed, not able to control myself and I could tell Passion was taking advantage of our little bonding moment as she continued.

"Champagne, now you know a nigga who getting money fa'real not about to have his main bitch walking around smelling like seafood, all day every day." I was laying in my bed, imagining women walking up to Passion and confronting her about messing with their men. It wasn't like the old days where they would be ready to fight, now they were blowing bitches' brains out and I was praying it wouldn't be her downfall.

We continued talking another fifteen minutes as I explained the plan that I came up with from the information I got from Sweatt, pillow talking after I fed this pussy to him. I still had a couple loose ends to tie up, but everything was pretty much a green light. And with the payout of this scheme, Passion and I were on our way to living like El Capo's wife, and that meant fuck Mahogany and they ratchet ass Baller Babies.

Once Passion was out my room, I grabbed my personal items and made my way to the bathroom to take my morning shower. The whole time the water was massaging my body, my mind was wondering what the hell happened with Mahogany and Rue last night. She literally had his ass by the balls and then the next minute he escapes? Could her ass be playing games? She did fall for that nigga quicker than a cat could lick its ass and I just don't think she could hate him that fast, but then again, I do believe it's a thin line between love and hate.

I was wrecking my brain trying to figure out other people's problems, so I got out the shower, brushed my mouth and then got dressed in my bedroom before making my way to the living room.

"Come have a seat, Champagne, we need to have a family meeting," Mahogany stated as Passion and E'mani sat beside her with an expressionless look on their faces. I had no clue what the hell was going on, but usually when there's a meeting called, somebody fucked up. I sat down in the La-Z-Boy chair across from them, with my hands in my lap so I would have easy access to the gun I kept under the cushion if I needed it. Nobody's safe in these situations, so I wasn't taking any chances.

"Allow me to start this meeting off by saying, nothing goes unnoticed in this family and when you fuck up, own up to it and take your punishment like the boss bitch you are. I'm no exception, so I would like to take this time to admit that I fucked up last night." She looked each one of us in the face as she paused, I guess to see if we had anything to say, but I was all ears and wanted to know what really happened.

"Once Rue and I disappeared into the room, he wasted no time trying to apologize for the pain he caused me, but I silenced him by planting kisses all over his face as I stripped him naked. I then laid him on his back as I licked down his body until I was face-to-face with his manhood, which I made disappear into my mouth like magic. I reached for my gun at this time but was enjoying the feeling of him down my throat so much, I failed to go for the kill.

"It was at that moment that we both heard the sound of gunshots and Rue spotted my gun before knocking me to the ground, making me lose sight of it. We tussled while at the same time scrambled to find it and by the grace of God, I came out on top. But by the time I looked up, all I saw the back of his naked body as he ran out the room."

We sat there quiet and looking stupid at each other, even after she was done telling us what happened.

"I mean, neither of you going to say anything?" Mahogany asked and then looked at me. "What about you, Champagne? You had a lot to say last night. I guess the cat got your tongue, huh?" I still said nothing, honestly what was there to say we just had to make sure we stay on safe mode, so we don't lose our lives. We all agreed there would be no punishment for Mahogany, even though she claimed she would accept her shit like a boss.

At times, I really do think Mahogany just be talking because she can. I mean, yeah, I've heard the stories about what happened between her and the Bloods and then later with the Crips at the Florida Institution for Teenage Girls. But that's all they are, stories. And let's not forget, that shit took place over five years ago.

Once it was announced the meeting was over, my phone rang, snatching my attention just as Passion mouthed the words, *Palm Beach*. I shook my head yeah as I held up my index finger and then walked out the door to take my call. In my car, I rapped along with

Plies and bopped my head as I turned the volume up to the max. I had two twelve-inch subwoofers in the trunk, so I was loving how the bass was booming. It was times like this that made a bitch want to pop off on Molly because one, I been horny as hell lately and wasn't getting no dick, which can cause stress and two, I was tired of being around emotional ass bitches, Passion included.

They all thought I left out the house to take a phone call, when in actuality, I had my phone set to ring so I would have a reason to get away from their asses. I was so caught up in myself, I never saw Mahogany standing at my car door, until she banged on the window. I wanted to ignore her, but she knew I saw her.

"What the fuck is wrong with you, banging on my shit like that?" I asked before she had a chance to say anything once I let the window down. She looked at me as if I had two heads before she contributed to our shouting match.

"You need to turn that damn music down. You're not in the damn projects of Gainesville anymore, so you need to have some fuckin respect. We do have neighbors!" I really didn't feel like going back and forth with her, because everybody knew Mahogany had to be right about everything, so I turned the volume down.

"Are you done yet?" I asked sarcastically and the minute she didn't respond, I threw my car in drive and took off, not really knowing where the hell I was going. I just drove and drove but once I got to the interstate, my plan was to turn around until I saw the unmarked police car with the flashing red and blue lights behind me. I pulled over after doing a quick search of my car to make sure I didn't have anything illegal. I should be alright, because my driver's license was good and I didn't break the law. Well, at least I thought I didn't.

"Driver, turn off the engine and drop the keys outside the window now!" the officer said through their car grill speaker. I did as I was told, thinking this was the normal traffic stop procedure they used in Tampa. And also because I knew the authorities had a problem with believing Black Lives Matter and wouldn't hesitate to pull the trigger on a person of color, man or woman.

"Now slowly reach both hands out the window and proceed to open the car door from the outside, slowly." I continued to follow the orders that were given to me and by the time I was face down on the ground, I felt the weight of the cold steel bracelets around my wrist. I was looking around for anybody with a cell phone that might be recording, in case my luck suddenly turned worse and the bitch who was detaining me got trigger happy.

I was taken to the federal holding building which was something like a precinct but run by the FBI. They kept me in this freezing cold room for at least two hours before somebody even showed up to talk to me and I couldn't even say I was upset, because I was more than that. I was pissed the fuck off.

"Good afternoon, Ms. Jamison. Sha'nay Jamison, right? Well, I'm Agent Watson with the Federal Bureau of Investigation and I have a proposition I think you would be interested in taking," the officer holding me against my will stated as if this was our first time meeting over a casual lunch. I stared at her thinking, *this bitch has to be crazy*, before shaking my head and smiling at her face.

"I don't know what y'all expected from the citizens in Tampa, but where I'm from we don't do business with opposition, which is anybody who has a badge, so you don't have anything I'm interested in."

She smiled back at me with a little too much confidence in her posture and I could tell right then she had something up her sleeves. "I figured you would say something of that nature, so I brought with me what I call 'something that will get your mind right,'" she responded, before pulling out a folder with a variety of pictures, and the second my eyes focused on them, my breath got caught in my throat.

Keith Williams

Chapter 19

E'mani

"Everybody on the fuckin floor!" we heard after the door was kicked opened with so much force, the doorknob smashed into the wall, leaving a hole. I was so fucking scared that I played possum, not moving a muscle because I knew it was Rue coming back to get revenge. Who else was bold enough to run up in our shit like that? Passion, on the other hand, I hope was doing the same because I would hate to witness her life being taken by this muthafucka. I peeped from under my blanket as he moved towards her with his gun raised and I began to pray as I never did before.

Afraid God wouldn't answer me, I reached for my burna just as Passion swiftly pulled her right hand from under her pillow, gripped a pearl handle .25 caliber handgun and slid it under his nuts. I was so thankful for her boldness because I could tell she caught him completely by surprise as he felt the heavy steel, and that's when I made my move by coming up behind him with my .22 Ruger aimed at the left side of his temple.

"Drop that shit or I'ma blow your fuckin head off," Passion said through clenched teeth as I gave the handle of my gun a tighter squeeze, ready to catch another body.

"Hold up! Hold up, it's me," we heard him say as he dropped his gun and snatched off his mask. Surprised was an understatement of how we felt when our intruder turned out to be Mahogany's brother, Sweatt.

"What the fuck was that about? We could've killed you, playing games like that," I said, still gripping my burna in my hand. He claimed Mahogany told him everything that went down with Rue the other day and he was just making sure we were alright. If anybody asked me, I think that was just the excuse he gave because his little game didn't turn out like he planned. Or, was he really serious with that lame ass plan to rob us? Once he noticed that Mahogany and Champagne weren't in the house, he left before telling us to let them know he was here.

I don't know what it was, but it was something I never liked about Sweatt and if it wasn't for the love I had for Mahogany, I swear he would've been another body under my belt. So many times, he had tried to fuck me while claiming he loved me like a sister in front of Mahogany. I walked in the kitchen after Passion as the thought of visiting my hometown crossed my mind. It had been awhile, and I sometimes missed the excitement.

"Passion, you know it's the Classic weekend. How you feel about going to Orlando to hang out?" I asked, eying her and hoping that she says she would love to go. The Classic was a rival football game between Bethune Cookman, and Florida A&M University, also known as FAMU. Two black colleges who were fighting to prove to the world that they were the best in the state of Florida. And let's not forget the car show, which alone made Orlando the spot to be for the whole weekend, and it was also known that people in the surrounding states sometimes planned this trip months in advance.

Passion eyed me back with a crazy expression on her face and didn't even have to say a word, because I already knew what she was thinking. Her ghetto ass ex-fiancé goes to the Classic every year and we both knew he was gone show his ass if she saw her, especially around so many dudes who were getting money.

"I really wanna go to get my mind off all the bullshit we been going through lately, but you and I both know Quelly crazy ass gone be there and I'm not tryna go to jail fuckin around with that nigga," she responded as she twisted up her face, like just the thought of him made her mad. I don't really know what I was expecting her to say, but it damn sure wasn't the shit that came out of her mouth and it made me feel some type of way.

"You know what, fuck you! I don't need you to go with me anyway. I don't know why I even asked," I snapped, not even knowing why. She looked at me confused, before exploding in my face like I knew she would. We were now barking at each other like pit bulls, but deep down inside we knew not to cross the other's line.

After a while, I got tired of arguing and got my clothes to go take a hot bath. The hot water and body wash left my skin feeling smooth and soft as I rubbed up and down my legs and thighs slowly. I then lay back, resting my head on the end of the tub deep in thought. I knew I was wrong for what I said and how I acted. All she was doing was keeping it real with me but hey, I can't change what was already done.

"You should've known better than to think I would leave. You should've known your girl was gonna ride or die…" The sound of my ringing cell phone broke my train of thought. I checked the screen and noticed a text message from Dontay, telling me that I was on his mind. I smiled, placing the phone to my chest next to my heart, before sliding it back under my towel. I was quickly starting to feel something for Dontay, I don't know if it was love or if it was just the sex, but it was something.

After thirty long minutes, I got out the tub, dried off then exited with my towel wrapped around my body. I was hoping Passion would be asleep so I wouldn't have to hear her mouth anymore, but to my surprise, I walked in on her sitting on the floor naked, while snorting a white powder off the coffee table.

"What the hell you doing?" I shouted in shock. She just looked at me and smiled like a confused Chinaman.

"I'm making myself feel good," she said, getting up off the floor. "You wanna try some? I swear, it will help you relax and forget about all the drama." I had never done any drugs before, but low-key always wondered how it would make me feel. Passion took another line up her nose, then rubbed some along the outside her gumline. She then made a thinner one before pushing it closer to me to clean up, but I had no idea what to do, so I did exactly as I saw her do. I held down my right nostril and snorted half the line with my left.

"Finish the whole line," she encouraged me. I did as I was told, before going into a sneezing fit as my nose ran uncontrollably.

"Why is my nose running like this?" I asked, afraid I would die because I didn't do something right.

"It's called a drain, all you have to do is tilt your head back and let it drain down your throat," Passion coached me. I did as she said and the feeling I felt was like nothing I had ever felt before. I took another hit, this time using my right nostril and I was so high, it felt like I was floating in the sky as I felt Passion pull my towel off and lap her tongue across my nipples, but I didn't stop her.

Mmmm... wha... what are you doing?" I moaned as she continued to suck my breasts and softly bite my nipples. She led me to the couch and lay me on my back. I wanted to stop her so bad because this wasn't me. I didn't fuck around like this, but the feeling was too good and it was like the coke made my body extra sensitive, while she was hitting all the right spots. *I can't believe I'm letting this bitch do this to me*, I thought as she spread my legs and pushed her face into my pussy. She then slipped two of her fingers inside me, stroking my G-spot while sucking my swollen clit and causing tidal waves of pleasure to flow through my body.

Ahhh... that feels so damn good," I continued to moan, while grinding my pussy against her face and hand. She started moving in and out of me slowly, only speeding up after hearing my moans of encouragement. But at the moment, only one thing would make me completely satisfied and forget about letting another woman eat my pussy, and it started with a "O" and ended with me having no more energy.

The way Passion was going at it, I knew it wouldn't be long, at least I thought. I continued laying on my back and stared at the ceiling as it felt like I was getting higher and higher once Passion finished taking me on a ride. The head she had given me was one in a million, and even though I wasn't into women, I found myself showing her my appreciation by giving her the same satisfaction she had given me. While she crawled on her hands and knees to feed her nose with more coke, I was right behind her, sticking my face in her pussy from behind. She moaned before pushing her ass back at me as I spread her lips with my thumbs and teased the bulging pearl of her clit.

"Mmmm... fuck, yeah!" She continued to let me know I was hitting her spots. I slid two of my fingers inside her soaking wet pussy, before moving them in a circular motion as I often did to myself when I was horny. I was aware of how much pleasure she was feeling without her having to say anything, because I knew the kind of satisfaction my hands were capable of causing.

After a while, I removed my hands and savagely licked from the top of her clit to the bottom of her ass, causing her to moan loudly, revealing the sensation she felt. Once I sucked her clit into my warm mouth before slowly twirling my tongue across it, she started climaxing like I've never seen before as her body shook uncontrollably.

Once I finished, I walked to my room and lay in my bed still feeling like I was lost in space, but ready to come down. I didn't want to think about what just happened with me and Passion, or that I might be a lesbian because I liked it, but the truth is that's exactly where my mind kept shifting to and it was like a nightmare.

My cell phone rang, and I swear it felt like it took me a whole hour just to answer, and I was surprised the caller didn't hang up. It was Dontay, wanting to see me and to keep myself from feeling guilty about what I just did, I told him I was on my way just to get him off the phone.

Once I got into my Beemer, my mind went to racing with a million thoughts as I was finally coming down from my high and started to feel normal again. I didn't know how this was going to affect my relationship with Passion, or even Mahogany and Champagne, but I was planning on taking this shit to my grave, believe that. I stopped at the light once it turned red and a smoke gray Dodge Charger with chrome rims crept up next to me, damn near side swiping me on the right.

I looked but couldn't see who the driver was, being that the windows were tinted black. Thinking this was Rue or one of his goons I grabbed my Ruger from under the seat and sat in on my lap for protection. The light turned green and I figured I had one or two choices. I could keep going, hoping they'd turn off at the next light, or I could handle my business and take my chance of confronting these muthafuckas with a shootout.

Without a second thought, I quickly chose option two, before stepping on the gas, taking off straight towards the BP gas station on the corner. I peeked out my rear-view mirror, but by the time I stopped, the Charger was swerving into my lane and headed straight at me. The second the driver hit the brakes, I threw my door open and jumped out with my burna in their face, ready to body me a bitch.

To my surprise, Champagne yelled, "Don't shoot!" at the right time, because I was so close to illustrating before I lowered my gun.

"What the hell is wrong with you?" I yelled through the open window at her. "Are you tryna get yourself killed out here, like fa'real?" She sat there quiet for about a minute I guess, until she built up the courage to say something.

"Bitch, you almost shot," she finally said. I really don't know what she was thinking, but I knew I wasn't wrong for pulling my burna, because I had no idea that she was driving the car. *Honestly, I was tryna save my own damn life*, I thought as I stared at her and shook my head, feeling sorry for her, because I knew she thought this was a fucking game.

"That's my bad, E'mani. I know we're all paranoid right now, not knowing when Rue will come after us, but I was just on my way home to pick up Passion because we have business to take care of out of town. I saw your car and wanted to have a little fun, but I really didn't mean to scare you like that."

I told her it was alright and not to worry about it because I really wanted to get away from her. I didn't want to take the chance that she'd talked to Passion already and found out our secret. That would be embarrassing as hell. Without further ado, I quickly wished her good luck on her business out of town and jumped back in my car. The rest of the way, I kept thinking about how I would tell Dontay. I mean, I know I said I would take this secret to my grave, but I just felt like I had to tell him and I really didn't think he would take too kindly of somebody else sampling his pussy, female or not.

"Something gotta give," I said as I jumped out at Publix grocery store to grab a couple personal items. The young cashier always flirted with me when I stopped by. So, whenever I bought anything and there would be change left over, which was always, I would tell him to keep it putting a big smile on his face.

"Thank you, pretty lady," he said in a flirtatious manner.

I gave him my million-dollar smile, showing all thirty-two of my teeth and told him, "You're welcome," before walking out the store and back to my car.

"Damn, I'm a bad bitch," I said to myself while staring into the rear-view mirror, before starting the car and pulling off to meet my future baby daddy.

"Welcome to the place where all your fantasies could come true, where nothing else matters but pleasing you. I'm him, so let me take you there and I'm yours, so you don't just have to stare," Dontay greeted me the second I walked into his house and admired his naked body. *Not again*, I thought as I tried my hardest to look away, but it seems this mission was impossible. This was about to be the second session today and I didn't think my kitty could take any more orgasms, but I was definitely about to find out whether I wanted to or not, because she was wetter than the floor of a bathroom that didn't have shower curtains.

Keith Williams

Chapter 20

Mahogany

"Congratulations, Ms. White!" the doctor told me with a huge smile on his face. "I'm happy to be the first to confirm you're going to be a mommy. You're six and a half weeks pregnant." I could still hear the doctor's words in my head as I sat on my bed with my feet folded under me Indian style. I was waiting on E'mani to come home so we could have our sister-to-sister talk.

"This is crazy," I said, smiling to myself to keep from spazzing the fuck out. I wanted to be happy I was pregnant, but at the same time I couldn't enjoy the moment, because the secret of my past hunted me. Hopefully today I would be able to let it all out to E'mani without her judging me.

"Mahogany! I'm home and I hope whatever it is you have to tell me is important, because you just made me get off some dick to come home," E'mani yelled as she walked through the door. I heard her but couldn't say a word, because I still hadn't got over the shock of everything. "Mahogany!" she yelled again, this time walking into my room like she owned the muthafucka.

"What the fuck is you doing all that damn yelling for? I'm not deaf," I responded. We both stared at each other for a couple seconds, before she gave me her big schoolgirl smile, while waiting on me to tell her the big news. I took a deep breath to calm my nerves and shook my head before spilling the beans everywhere.

"I'm six and a half weeks pregnant."

"Oh, my God! I knew you were pregnant! I knew it," she yelled excitedly, with her hands covering her mouth. "All that bullshit you were saying about not being able to have children, look at you now." I tried to smile to show I was happy, but E'mani saw right through me and knew something wasn't right.

"What's up with you, girl? You should be one of the happiest women on earth right now. You're about to bring another Baller baby into the world," she said with her smile slowly disappearing.

"Talk to me, what's going on with you?" I tried to hold back, but I couldn't stop the tears from falling down my face as I broke down.

"I don't know if it's Rue's baby."

"What!" she yelled. "What you mean you don't know if it's Rue's baby?" I broke down even more, crying like a damn toddler before telling her the secret of why I didn't know whose baby I was carrying.

"Do you remember everything I told you happened with Rue? Well, what I didn't tell you was that when I left the house, I wanted to get back at him. So, I met the guy I liked and we went back to his place." I stopped for a minute to look her in the eyes before continuing. "And we had sex, unprotected."

"Oh, my fuckin God! How fuckin stupid can you be to move off your emotion like that? You didn't hurt Rue by going out to fuck somebody else, you hurt yourself because now you have to deal with the consequences of your actions," she responded, shaking her head while making me feel even worse.

"Everything that happened between me and this other guy was a mistake and I regret it ever happened. But now I really feel fucked up about it, because I don't even know his name. Please promise me you won't tell anybody about this, not even Champagne or Passion," I said on the verge of tears again. E'mani got up off the bed, looked herself over in the full-length mirror behind the door, before pulling me to my feet and hugging me tight.

"Out of all the crazy shit in the world you've done, this is by far the worse I know about. Not only did you fuck a complete stranger, you didn't even have the sense to use protection. But, looking past all that, you still my sister, it's Double B's forever and I'll never betray you. I promise you that." We both embraced each other in another tight hug for what seemed like hours before letting go.

"Lil bitch, you can't fuck with me if you wanted to, these expensive these is red bottoms, these is bloody shoes," Cardi B yelled through my cell phone as it rang. I looked to see who was calling and fucking up our bonding moment before noticing it was a text message from Rue.

"You tried to take me out, so I guess that means all is fair in love and war. But one thing I've learned from you is that I had to think outside the box, so right now I'm on my way to Palm Beach to get this brick mason money and I won't forget to let them know you sent me."

My breath got caught in my throat and I started hyperventilating as I read the message over and over again, before the phone slipped from my hand and hit the floor.

"I know he's not saying what I think he's saying," I kept repeating to myself as I started feeling lightheaded.

"Mahogany, what's going on?" E'mani asked while cupping my face in her hands so we were looking each other in the eyes. I remained silent as I saw my life flash before my eyes and my unborn child not giving a chance to bless this world with its presence. I didn't want that, neither did I want my brother Sweatt, the only brother I had left, to suffer behind something he had no knowledge of.

"Mahogany!" she screamed, this time bringing me back to the reality of this crazy world. I rushed to pick up my phone and called Champagne, before telling E'mani to ready because we were about to take another field trip. She looked confused and dumbfounded all at the same time, before opening her mouth and saying the dumbest shit I've ever heard.

"What, it's time for the baby?"

Oh, my fuckin God, I wanted to curse and scream at her ass so bad, but I knew that wouldn't get us anywhere, so politely as I could, I told her, to "Get your burna's and meet me in the car."

Champagne's phone kept ringing and ringing which were pissing me off even more and the minute I called Passion, her shit went straight to the voicemail.

"What the fuck is going on?" I yelled out of frustration, on the verge of throwing my phone against the wall like an idiot. I made it to the car and got in without saying a word. Literally, I think we only had about thirty minutes to get where we were going, so I wasted no time doing damn near the whole dashboard of 140 down

I-95. The first chance I got, I tried Champagne and Passion's phones again but got the same result as before, while I swerved through traffic like I was tryna elude the police. Every time I switched lanes, I came close to causing an accident because I didn't care who I was cutting off, that was until I reached the city limits of Palm Beach and the authorities tried to pull me over.

"Fuck!" I shouted as I pulled over to figure out what my next move would be.

"Driver, out of the car and get out with your hands in the air, now!" the officer yelled through the loudspeaker. I looked over at E'mani who was in the passenger seat all calm and I thought, *I never meant for my sister and me to get caught up like this, but if it's meant for us to go then so be it, because on everything I love, I swear we're going out like some real fuckin gangsta bitches. The streets gone remember us.*

I then told her, "Put on your seat belt," before flooring the gas pedal like my feet weighed a ton. We were doing close to eighty miles per hour as I flew down Old Dixie Highway, with two Palm Beach squad cars on my bumper. Approaching 25th and Pleasant City, I quickly pulled the E-brake and hit a sharp right going towards Spruce. The sirens from the squad cars had everybody from 25th to 15th at the side of the road cheering for us, not knowing who we were, just happy the police hadn't caught us yet.

I continued down Spruce Street, then hit a hard left by the old pool hall, side swiping two cars. The police were so close behind us, the minute they attempted the left turn, they drove right into incoming traffic, causing an eight-car pile-up. I peeped to my right and could see E'mani looking out the back window as cars flipped and ran into each other. I couldn't tell how bad the damage was, but when I saw E'mani bow her head in the prayer position, I knew it was serious.

Damn, I didn't intend for innocent people to get hurt, I thought as I drove for another ten minutes before turning into my destination.

"Where are we?" E'mani wanted to know as she looked around, not recognizing the place. I looked at her and at that moment, I realized I still hadn't told her what was going on. I quickly explained everything, from me pillow talking with Rue, to the text message I received today. I needed her to understand the type of danger Rue could put us in, so it was ride or die at this point. Once we were both on the same page, we got the car and cautiously walked towards the front door. The whole frame was barely hanging on and that let me know Rue was definitely here.

We continued inside as we both made our way up the staircase and while I entered the first door on the left of the hallway, E'mani checked the one on the far right. I walked in, expecting to catch Rue or any of his people by surprise and end their life with a bullet to the head, but what I saw put even more fear in my heart, because I knew my death certificate was already signed. Passion had Mr. Montoya facing the wall at gunpoint, while three bodies with masks covering their faces lay in the middle of the floor motionless.

"Passion, what the fuck are you doing?" I asked with my gun aimed at her. At the sound of my voice, they both turned to face me and that's when I saw the blood trailing down Mr. Montoya's face from the gash on the side of his head. She stared without saying a word, I guess more surprised to see me than I was to see her as I tried to move closer. The second I took another step, she drew a second gun and aimed at me as if I was now the enemy.

"I don't want to do it, Mahogany. But I swear, if you make another move, I will body your ass," she declared like I was a complete stranger trying to harm her.

"This is what it now come down to? You're willing to risk the lives of the people you call family for drugs and money, huh?" I said, more so trying to save face with Mr. Montoya than anything. She never answered and what pissed me off even more was the way Mr. Montoya glared at me, because I knew he was thinking I set all this up.

"Bitch, answer me when I'm talking to you. All the shit I've done for you and that bitch, Champagne, I brought you into my family, showed you love like no other and this how you disrespect me?

Bitch, fuck you," I shouted, losing my cool and before I knew it, her eyes grew wide with shock as bullets raced at her, lifting her body off the ground and throwing her against the wall and killing her. Mr. Montoya quickly scrambled for her gun and by the time Passion's body hit the floor, we were already having a standoff.

I tried pleading with Mr. Montoya, but he had no understanding. He felt like I betrayed his trust and caused harm to him and his family by barging into his home. We went back and forth like a married couple, and his word was usually bond. But not one single shot was fired as we stood with our guns drawn, and that let me know there was still doubt in his mind that I didn't have anything to do with this. I tried convincing him to lower his gun as I was going to do the same, but he wouldn't and I feared if I gave him any leeway, he would take advantage of me.

"Ms. White, are you in here?" I heard my name before seeing the face behind the voice. Mr. Montoya looked at me confused, as I did the same because I had no idea who it could be, and I wanted to be prepared in case it was an enemy. I stepped closer to the life sized statue of the Virgin Mary, in case I needed to take cover, as a female entered the room cautiously with her gun drawn. She said my name again, only this time she spotted Mr. Montoya and me at our standoff, before waving her gun back and forth between me and him.

"What do we have here? It looks to me like I missed out on all the fun," she said, looking around the room at the bodies lying on the floor. "Well, better late than never. Old man, out!" Mr. Montoya smiled, but didn't move. I knew he wasn't used to taking orders from women, but once he realized how serious she was, he quickly turned his back to us before making his way towards the door.

Personally, I thought that was the dumbest mistake anybody could ever make, I would never take my eyes off a person this close to me with a gun in their hand. Mr. Montoya never had a chance to think about it, because the minute he grabbed the doorknob, fragments of his brain flew everywhere from the result of her sending two bullets to his head at point-blank range. I jumped back stunned, while at the same time trying to avoid the mess of blood contaminating the room.

"Now that I have your attention, please allow me to introduce myself. My name is Agent Daniesse Watson with the Federal Bureau of Investigation, and I'm a pissed-off bitch who's dying for revenge against you," she said with a wicked grin on her face.

I knew this day would creep up on me, after all the shit I've done. I wouldn't feel right if it didn't, but I frowned because I had no idea who this bitch was, or what the hell I've done to her.

"Oh, that's so cute, you really look lost. Well, allow me to refresh your memory. the people you killed to help free E'mani Newman were my family. Yes, Judge Lester Wright was my father and Ashlyn and Alice Wright were my sisters. You killed them in cold blood, before burning down the house. But that's not the only reason I want you dead, you also murdered my husband, Jermaine Watson."

I kept my mouth closed with a lost look on my face as we continued our standoff. I just knew this bitch wasn't talking about who I think she was talking about. I shook my head no because it couldn't be. That would mean everything we had was a lie and I knew it wasn't, I knew it was all real. Then, she interrupted my thoughts with the confirmation I was looking for, which pissed me the fuck off.

"You might know him as Supreme, but you took him away from me and our five-year-old son, so now you have to die," she said, before I saw a flash and heard multiple shots ring out. The only thing I regretted was not asking the man up above for forgiveness.

Keith Williams

Chapter 21

E'mani

I really didn't know what to expect as I slowly walked toward the far end of the hallway to see what was behind door number two. I could say fuck it and just go in like Rambo, but then I might hit one of Mr. Montoya's people and the way Mahogany talked about him, that was something I damn sure didn't want to do. The other option I had was to try sneaking in without anyone noticing me, but the minute I heard gunshots I forgot all about any plans I had in the making and burst through the door to the sight of Rue and Champagne having a shootout as if they had been lifetime enemies.

My first instinct was to end everything with a bullet to the back of Rue's head, but I guess the energy of my presence could be felt, because Rue turned around with his gun blazing. I jumped out the way a split second before I was to meet my maker, but somehow a bullet still managed to graze the right side of my face as I stumbled to the wall. Champagne yelled, firing shot after shot from her twelve-gauge, leaving the whole room smelling of burning wood as she hit everything but her intended target.

I knew she was probably thinking I was hit bad but the way this shit was burning, that's exactually how it felt. Rue had already dropped to the floor and probably crawled to the other side of the bed to take cover. Once the shots stopped, Champagne walked around the bed to finish what she started thinking Rue was wounded but got a hell of a surprise when she got there. Rue was nowhere to be found. At least, we didn't see him.

"What the fuck?" she whispered to herself but loud enough to where I could still hear her as he scratched her head. I could tell she was confused, but then she looked at me and I guess it hit her, there was only one place he could be. She leaned over the bed trying to get my attention, and everything happened so damn fast, it felt like I lost myself. Rue sent three shots straight through the mattress from under the bed, with every last one of them connecting with Champagne's body and throwing her backwards.

She slid down the wall before taking her last breath, and I lost it as I shredded the whole mattress with every shot I had in my gun, after witnessing Champagne's body hit the floor. Once my gun clicked, indicating that I was out of bullets, I threw it to the side before grabbing Champagne's twelve-gauge and continued feeding the mattress all the lead I had.

If he wasn't dead after that, then I knew God had something else planned for him, but I didn't think twice about it as I ran towards Champagne's motionless body before dropping to my knees. I had so many mixed feelings, I didn't know what to do. I mean, I really didn't know her that well, so why the hell was I so in my feelings? But then again, the time we did have were all memorable and I was starting to love her like a sister.

Damn, I hated this part of life, I thought as I ran my hands down her face to close her open eyes. I said a quick prayer for her family, before making my way back to the hallway once I thought about Mahogany.

I didn't know how I was going to break everything down to Mahogany. She had a closer bond with Champagne, so I knew I had to say something. I leaned against the door contemplating what I would say as my hand rested on the doorknob. Again, I hated this part of life. A couple minutes passed as my mind ran wild, but I ended up losing my train of thought when I heard a voice that wasn't Mahogany's, one sounded really familiar.

I eased the door open without being noticed and the sight of that bitch Agent Watson, brought back memories of her threatening me with life in prison if I didn't snitch on Mahogany. The bitch needed to be right in the fucking ground, with the rest of her family, and I was just the person to do it. I reached for my gun but kept my eyes on her and Mahogany. Something wasn't right, I questioned myself. *Where the fuck is my burna*, I thought as it hit me that I tossed it after I ran out of bullets. Damn I wanted to kick myself in the ass for not being fully prepared.

I hurried back down the hall and the minute I stepped into the room I ran to grab Rue's gun from under the bed. It was covered in blood and smelled of iron, but I didn't care as I made my way back to handle my business. Agent Watson was still talking, and I couldn't believe what I walked up on when she said Supreme was her husband and the father of her five-year-old son. *What the fuck*, I thought, getting frustrated. He was still fucking me and Mahogany five years ago, and just the thought of him playing me like he did, made me want to kill this bitch even more.

I tried getting Mahogany's attention before I started shooting, but she wouldn't look my way, and I felt like time wasn't on our side. Every second that passed I wanted to end her life faster for Mahogany and me, until I finally received the opportunity. Mahogany took a step before shifting her attention my way and I walked through the threshold, unloading the .45 caliber I held gripped in my hand until Agent Watson's body hit the floor.

Somewhere between me standing over Agent Watson's body and checking to see if she were dead, Mahogany snatched the gun away from me and sent two more shots to her head at point-blank range to make sure she was dead, at least that's what she told me. Paralyzed by the thought of everything finally being over, Mahogany and I both stood there until things got occult. This was not the life I wanted to live anymore, it came with too much death and I've come close to losing my life twice. We needed to do better, especially with the baby Mahogany was carrying, it deserved better than what we would provide living this lifestyle.

I got ready to voice what I was thinking when the loud sounds of police sirens and doors being kicked in broke my train of thought. Mahogany and I once again stared at each other before she told me to run. I didn't move because I didn't want to leave her to take the fall for everything that happened tonight, but the boss bitch in her wouldn't have it any other way.

"E'mani! What you waiting for? Get the fuck out of here, they're coming."

"No!" I shouted as tears started down my face. "I'm not leaving you, either they get both of us or none of us." She grabbed my face to wipe away my tears as her own began to fall and then hugged me tight. This was the side of Mahogany many people never got a chance to see. She wasn't always a bitch, or plotting to kill somebody as people claimed, she really did have a soft spot in her heart for the people she cared about.

"Listen, E'mani, you have to go there's no reason for both of us to die here tonight and besides, the streets will be a safer place without me anyway," she responded, sounding like she was trying to make a joke out of the situation, but I really didn't see a damn thing about this shit funny.

"That baby deserves a chance, Mahogany, you owe it that much—"

"And because of that reason, I won't hold court in the streets," she replied, cutting me off before pushing me towards the window as the door came crashing in. I made it out the house without being noticed by the agents but stayed close enough to where I could see how they manhandled Mahogany. They threw her on the floor and roughly cuffed her hand behind her back, not once taking into consideration that she was a woman. I swear, I wanted to kill every last one of them with a bullet to the head, and then watch their families cry. Once they started to escort her out, I took off running and running, without knowing where I was going or what I would do in this foreign city.

Chapter 22

E'mani

Dontay and I both sat in the front row of the courtroom as we waited on them to bring Mahogany out and I can't lie, I really felt sorry for her. The news portrayed her as a fucking monster, who didn't give a damn about human life, and a person who would kill just for the sport of it. They even said this was the worst case of homicides in the history of Palm Beach County by a female, giving her the record of ten bodies, which I knew for a fact wasn't true because there wasn't even ten muthafuckas in the house.

Four different news station camera crews were stationed all around the courtroom to get the perfect view of the infamous Ms. Mahogany White, for the top story that could probably make their careers. The bailiff shouted, "All rise," as the judge made his way from his chamber and it was that moment, I saw the two Cuban men in suits, one looking like the splitting image of Mr. Montoya. I looked at Dontay to see if he thought the same thing, forgetting that he had no idea what Mr. Montoya looked like, so it would be a waste of time confiding in him about it.

I kept my eyes on them to find out who they were here to see, because they stood out like a sore thumb. The first person they brought to the podium was a white man who looked like he could be a character from the show, *The Walking Dead*. His skin was dirty, he had acne on his face so bad it was starting to look like a rash, and I could tell he didn't believe in brushing his teeth, because his mouth looked like it was full of mold. He was being charged with occupying a meth lab, and even after reading off all his priors, the judge still set his bail at only twenty thousand dollars before sending him on his way.

The next person they brought out was a fifty-something-year-old black man who looked as if he was actually fifteen years younger. He was freshly groomed, had swagger like he didn't have a care in the world, and he had two white men beside him, ready to fight whatever charges he was being accused of. The judge read off the charges of two counts of fraud by wire transfer, one count of money laundering over one hundred thousand dollars, and two counts of identity fraud, before he looked up from his paperwork like he couldn't believe what he was reading. I couldn't believe it my damn self and I now felt like I was in the wrong line of business, because the way his lawyers were prepared, I didn't think he would spend another night in jail.

The lawyers did their thing as they spoke, and the judge replied. I had no idea of what was actually being argued, but it sure didn't take long for the judge to decide he was setting the man free on his own recognizance, to fight the charges from the streets. I wanted to clap because so far, it looked as if a black man was beating the system, which is something you didn't see too often and that really made me proud. Dontay also looked surprised, because by him working for the county jail, he saw black men and women get railroaded all the time.

They finally brought Mahogany out and cameras started flashing everywhere as she held her head up. She smiled when she saw me, but I couldn't smile back, because it hurt me to my heart to see my sister like this. She looked bad. I mean, her hair was matted on her head, she had bags under her eyes and looked as if she hadn't slept since she was arrested. And I could see the stress weighing her down like a bad disease. I was praying the baby was alright, because she also looked like she hadn't been eating, which I hated to think about.

Mr. Conn walked through the door right as Mahogany stepped to the podium and he looked as if he came to fight. They smiled at each other and then Mr. Conn gave me a head nod, before giving his attention to the judge as he read over Mahogany's case. He basically confirmed what the news had been broadcasting, but he went a little deeper as to revealing the names of all the victims.

One by one, he read off the names and the minutes he said, "Alex Montoya," I looked at the two Cuban men in the suits as they both nodded their heads at each other, letting me know they were here to identify Mahogany.

It sent a cold chill through my body, because now I was really worried about Mahogany's safety but then again, she might be alright because they had her on protected custody, due to the status of her case. The two Cuban men left the courtroom right as the judge told Mr. Conn he was crazy to think Mahogany deserved a bond and then hit his gavel after announcing all chances of her ever-seeing daylight again were denied.

Mahogany kept her head up as they escorted her to the back, but I wanted to cry. I wanted to cry for her because she was too tough to cry for herself, I wanted to cry for her because she was too young to lose her life to this corrupted system, and I wanted to cry because I was losing the only person that wasn't related to me by blood, but remained my sister through loyalty. Dontay hugged me as we also got up to leave, he didn't know Mahogany that well, so this didn't affect him too much. I'm thinking he was only worried about me and how this would affect me mentally and physically.

The minute we walked out the front door of the courthouse, reporters from different news stations rushed us and pushed their mics in our faces as they started drilling us with questions like the disrespectful muthafuckas they are.

"Who's the leader of the notorious Baller Babies, now that Ms. White have been captured like a wild animal?"

"Ms. Newman, is this your new boyfriend and will he be next on the list to become your victim as Mr. Watson aka Supreme was?"

One reporter even had the nerve to ask me would I testify on Mahogany if I were called as a witness by the prosecutor. I wanted to break every last camera out there and was on my way to doing just that, until Dontay grabbed me into a bear hug and escorted me past them like he was my security guard, and without answering anyone of their questions. How the hell did they even know I was part of the Baller Babies? And then, I hated that Dontay had to hear all that shit they said about Supreme. I looked over at him as he drove before apologizing.

"Stop, E'mani, you do not have to apologize for something that happened in the past. I know you wouldn't kill anybody without a reason, so the shit them reporters were asking about went in one ear and out the other," Dontay explained, making me feel better about the situation. We drove back to the house in Tampa, which is where Dontay had been staying with me since the day I made it back home.

I tried to relax, but every channel I turned to was talking about Mahogany's case or showed Dontay and I coming out of the court-house with a headline that read, "Last member of the Baller Babies." I wanted to scream so loud because I was now known to the whole state and would never get the chance to live a normal life again. I tried to take a quick nap as I lay on the couch, because all the chaos was starting to take a toll on me, but my ringing cell phone ended that. I answered on the third ring, well, what I thought was the third ring.

"You have a collect call from an inmate at the Palm Beach County Jail. To accept the charges, press one, to deny the charges press two and to block—" Before the automated system had a chance to finish talking, I pressed one.

"How you holding up?" I asked soon as I heard her say hello. She claimed she was doing good, but I could hear in her voice she wasn't and that made me feel even more fucked up, being that she was taking the charges for both of us.

"Listen, E'mani, they weren't gone stop coming after us until they got me. Haven't you noticed that once Supreme's life had been taken, it was war against us? First, his sister Ja'mya and that back-stabbing bitch Kayla, and then his stank pussy wife Agent Daniesse Watson, so don't beat yourself up or stress over all this bullshit be-cause I did it for us. Double B's," Mahogany explained, without saying too much to incriminate herself.

"I really didn't know how I would survive without you," I re-vealed and the only feedback she gave was that she had faith in me to keep her name and legacy alive. Well, all I thought at that mo-ment was that she had more faith in me then I had in myself, because I couldn't see what she saw. I then asked about the baby.

"Well, the nurses say the baby seems to be okay and growing without any problems, thank God. The other thing is I found out that no matter how long it takes for my case to get handled, they won't be able to send me to prison until after I have the baby." She sounded like that made her little excited. I mean, there's nothing excited about going to prison or even jail, not even a little bit. She was really handling all this bullshit like a boss bitch though, or she was just good at suppressing her true feelings and making it look like something it's not.

We continued talking and she told me something that blew my mind. She said it was even more surprising to her, but at the same time it was kind of exciting to see her mother walk into the visiting room. It had been a long ten years since they'd seen each other and like everybody else, her mother said she saw her on the news. She told me while talking that they cried, reminisced and then cried again, before her mother apologized to her for not being the mother that she needed her to be. She was starting to make me cry as I listened to her tell the story. *Damn, this was going to be hard without Mahogany*, I thought.

"You have one-minute left," the automated system announced, interrupting our conversation.

"Damn, that was a quick fifteen minutes," she said, sounding disappointed we didn't have long before the phone hung up. I really didn't want to hang up either, because it had been a long time since Mahogany and I was able to have a sentimental conversation without arguing, and I missed that.

I told her to call any time before the words, "I love you," came out my mouth.

She replied, "Ditto," right as the line got disconnected. It was times like this that made me want to say fuck the world with no lubrication, because I was just thinking about everything and I couldn't figure out how the hell they're going to prosecute Mahogany, when they didn't have any fucking witnesses.

"Bae, Mr. Wacko say he really misses you," Dontay said, referring to the nickname he gave his dick as he stood in front of me naked, holding it in his hand. I just looked at him like I was lost because for one, he just interrupted my fucking thoughts and two, I really wasn't in the mood to have sex. I mean, I was nowhere near wet and my mind was too focused on other shit to even try to get close to it.

"Dontay, you can get that thing out of my face, because I'm not in the mood," I replied, moving Mr. Wacko to the side like he meant nothing to me. Besides, he wasn't even hard anyway. I silently laughed to myself once Dontay walked off, not because I was picking on Mr. Wacko for being limp, but because I knew I would probably be on my knees apologizing to him later. I was now back to square one. Again, bored as all outdoors and sending my mind on a roller coaster ride, thinking about how I would help Mahogany out of the situation she's in.

BOOM! BOOM! BOOM! BOOM!

POP! POP! POP!

Du-Du-Du-Du-Du! Du-Du-Du-Du-Du!

What the fuck is going on, I thought as I walked to the window and peeped out. All I could hear were gunshots as the whole hood let round after round, off in the sky for the Fourth of July as they celebrated our independence. If this was my old neighborhood, that would've been a quick way to get hit with a stray bullet, but it wasn't, so I was okay. I had forgotten all about the holiday with Mahogany's case being fresh on my mind, and that's something that didn't happen often.

"Cuzzo, pass me the choppa!" I heard a man yell over all the loud gunshots. Once he received it, I swear it seemed like he let off fifty rounds in fifteen seconds as the night turned brighter. My phone started ringing and vibrating at the same time, grabbing my attention. I reached for it off the couch and without looking at the screen, which was starting to become a habit, I answered.

"Who dis?"

"I know you think you got away, but you haven't. We will find you and kill you, the way you did Montoya—"

"Man, who the fuck is this playing on my phone?" I asked again, this time getting upset, as I cut them in the middle of their sentence.

"Just know the timer on your life is ticking," he responded before disconnecting the line.

176

Chapter 23

E'mani

It was July 10, 2019, and the Yuengling Center at the University of South Florida was filled with college graduates and their families, celebrating their special day. The decor was simple, black and green. Half the graduates wore green caps and gowns, while the other half wore black. Flowers were everywhere, balloons could be heard popping throughout the building and every seat was reserved.

It was like a zoo, though, once the ceremony started. Applause could be heard from every direction every time a graduate walked across the stage to receive their degree. This one particular side sounded like a stampede of bulls from all the yelling and stomping the audience did to support Dontay's cousins Kendra and Keira as they walked across the stage.

"That's my muthafuckin cousin right there y'all!" Dontay's youngest cousin Tee yelled out, and next to her Dontay had damn near the whole family present to support two of the baddest bitches in the building. Blue, BG, Junior, Tay Tay, Shuntel and Malissa were in the building. They yelled and screamed Kendra and Keira's name every chance they got, even though they had people looking at us like animals.

Once the ceremony ended and everybody was starting to leave, the girls found Dontay and me waiting for them by the door. They both hugged and kissed us on the cheeks, before thanking us for coming and bringing everybody.

"C'mon now, cousin, you crazy to think I would miss this day. I'm so fuckin proud of y'all and I always knew you both would make it. E'mani and I have a surprise for y'all outside," Dontay explained, probably feeling more excited than they did. We went all out for them when it came to their graduation gifts and they both knew we weren't cheap, so I know they were getting more excited by the second. I covered Kendra's eyes, while Dontay covered Keira's and we led them to their surprise.

"How far is it? Because it feels like y'all walking us across the state line," Kendra complained.

"Calm down, calm down, we're here. When I count to three, we're going to remove our hands and y'all tell us what y'all think," I said, eying Dontay and at the same time, we both counted. "One...two...three!" We lifted our hands and watched their reactions as they adjusted their eyes before the excited little girls in them came out.

"Oh my God! Thank you, cousin! Thank you, we love it," they both screamed before wrapping their arms around our necks for a hug. Dontay and I went all out when we purchased the two, fully loaded Infiniti's, resting on 22-inch Forgiato rims. Kendra and Keira were still young and plus they were females, so we didn't want to go too big on the size of the rims. The insides were blessed with two, ten-inch DCL TV monitors in the headrests, and a fifteen-inch monitor in the dashboard. The only thing different about the cars were the colors. One was red and the other sparkling white, like the color of champagne.

"This ain't the only surprise. I have a bigger one for y'all," Dontay confessed.

"C'mon now, cousin, what's bigger than getting a fully loaded Infiniti?" Keira asked while playing with her TV screen. I wanted to tell her, but that wouldn't be right, and then the way Dontay looked at me said more than enough. By this time, the rest of the crew had gone home, all but Tee. Her little fast ass was being fresh with some little boy, until Dontay literally made her go home. Kendra and Keira both jumped into their cars and followed Dontay and me as we led them downtown to a row of office buildings. Once there, I parked on the next street to keep them from spoiling this surprise.

"Now it's time to cover them eyes again," Dontay said, smiling. We repeated the same process as before and walked them until we were standing directly in front of the building they now owned. After counting to three again, we removed our hands and they both went crazy with excitement, tears falling and everything, and it made us feel good to see the joy they felt.

"Is this what I think it is?" Kendra asked in disbelief and I really mean disbelief. Dontay and I both confirmed everything by revealing the name in neon lights. We brought them their own building to start their career. The names on the building read, Davis and Davis, Attorneys at Law, with a red bow around the door.

"Oh! My! God!" Keira cried. "This is too good to be true." They both ran at us and again hugged us as if we would fly away if they let us go.

"No, the both of you are too good to believe, you both earned it always remember that," I responded. They ran and ripped off the bow before going inside where they were to pick out their office. Two days before, Dontay and I had gotten the whole building furnished with top-of-the-line furniture, from the mahogany wood desks to the adjustable, long back office chairs.

"We promise, we will do everything we have to do to make our business the number-one law practice in the city, then in the state," Keira said, trying to hold back her tears. While they both finished crying from all the excitement of the day, I stood there deep in thought. I had something heavy on my mind that I wanted to share with them. I knew they would support me when I told them, but what I didn't want to do was risk their futures. I asked Dontay if he could excuse us for a second, before telling him I needed to talk to the girls alone. He looked at all three of us with a glare, before walking out the front door like he had just been declared the weakest link. I then called both girls to sit with me at the round table, which would probably be where they would hold all their future meetings. Once I had their full undivided attention, I looked around one more time, before speaking on what had my mind wandering like a lost puppy.

"We all know the situation with Mahogany, so as of now I'm taking the position as head of the Baller Babies, because my sister wants me to keep her name and legacy alive. The only problem I have is that I'm the last member standing, and I can't do it by myself, so I'm asking for your help. I'm asking you two to become the newest members of the Baller Babies and I can guarantee you that you will not regret it.

"I know you're about to start the law practice, but that move will be all the better, because we need something legit, especially a law practice after all the blood that would be shed." I paused, just to imagine what they were thinking as I watched the expressions on their faces. "What y'all think about all that?" For a second, they both just stared at each other, I guess not knowing what to say. I know Kendra and Keira both loved being hands-on in the street life, but at the same time, I also knew that wasn't the career they wanted for themselves in the future.

"Growing up, I always admired Mahogany and the Baller Babies, because they were bad bitches who demanded respect and handled their business, no matter the situation. Now, I really don't think I'm built for it, but I'm honored and will do my best to keep Mahogany's name and legacy alive, while standing next to you and screaming Double B's," Kendra stated, before smiling at Keira to let her know that she was riding with me.

"If my sister ridin, then I'm ridin, and the thing about me is that my name speaks for itself. Just ask anybody about Lil Thug, so the Baller Babies got a winner recruiting me always remember that E'mani. And like my sister said, I always had so much respect for the Baller Babies and no disrespect, but I'm trying to make my own legacy as a Baller Baby," Keira said with a little too much arrogance for my liking, but I felt she didn't really mean no disrespect like she said. Once she finished, we all said the Baller Baby prayer before thanking God for this new beginning.

After another ten to twenty minutes of getting things in order with the law practice and their new positions as a Baller Baby, we met Dontay at the car before going our separate ways.

Once we left, I quickly suggested to Dontay that we go out to dinner instead of going home, because I was tired of being cooped up in the house like I was on punishment. Dontay agreed, but suggested he had a better idea. since I always talked about the relaxing sound of the beach, he wanted to have a sunset picnic of Chinese food next to the water. I was too excited to say the least and on the way to our destination, I stopped by my favorite Chinese restaurant and ordered an assortment of shrimp fried rice with extra shrimp. It was a perfect choice for the evening if anybody asked me.

Before we could make it to the water, we came upon a sand dune, topped by wooden walkways and benches, so people could sit and just look at the beach and enjoy the cool breeze. The walkway started about ten feet from a very busy street that ran parallel to the beach. I lay a blanket down at the base of the dune within fifty feet of the ramp that comes down from the top, because it was still light out as we sat down.

Dontay was a big flirt and I knew he loved my attention, so I took pride in myself and dressed in a way that was classy but would also make most bitches who were in my presence jealous. I poured some champagne and we toasted our evening together before spreading out the plates of food and began to eat. Although we needed to be mindful of our surroundings because I was still receiving threatening phone calls, we couldn't help being exhibitionists as far as showing our passion for one another is concerned.

We ate most of our food and drank about half the bottle of champagne before we begun caressing one another and engaging in our typical deep throat kissing. The remaining champagne got kicked over and the food pushed aside, but by that time, we were too turned on to care. We were both dressed simply, me in a low-cut Gucci top tied below my full breasts and a pair of fitted shorts. Dontay on the other hand, had on a pair of Robin's Jeans and a wife beater.

While we kissed, we began pulling off each other's clothes and it was only moments before we were completely naked. People were walking by in the sand, but we just didn't care as we knelt back and looked at each other. He lay me down and began slowly kissing my body all over, hesitating only slightly at my soft and sensitive aromatic bush, on his way to my toes. He knew this would really turn me on, especially when he stopped and visited my gorgeous breasts on the return trip. My nipples were large and dark, and I knew the velvety texture of my skin and the firmness of my flesh were enough to keep him happily kissing and sucking me.

But there was more to indulge in, and he soon proceeded back down the center of my torso. He then probed my belly button with the tip of his tongue, and teased his way down to my chocolate bush, which revealed the beauty of the moon just visible below the sunset. We were both afraid the police who patrolled regularly would either happen to walk by or be called to the scene by someone who were offended by our antics, but we were too far gone to even consider stopping. I could tell he was lost in the wonderful taste and smell of my pussy and wasn't about to relinquish me until I had been satisfied.

He always bragged that before he met me, women would tell him he was blessed when it came to using his tongue. I could tell he was applying what he had been told, because he was making my pussy talk when all this time, I thought she was a mute. He nibbled lightly on my swollen clit and before sliding his tongue inside me, I raised my hips to meet his tongue before he was back to teasing and licking my clit.

I was trying to hold off long as I could, but he wouldn't let me as he sucked on my clit harder and I was soon gushing oceans of love juice and writhing all over the blanket. Soon as I calmed down a bit, he kissed me while he held me close, after all it was love the kelp us together and the sex is so much more pleasurable when you're in love.

"Now, it's my turn," I moaned as I turned him over and let my mouth dance over his chest and stomach. I noticed his dick was throbbing by the time I teased my way down to it. I knelt between his legs and begun to suck the head of his dick, drawing out the pre-cum and relishing its taste. I then slid my hands under his butt and pulled him into my waiting mouth, while I alternated between encircling the tip with my tongue and driving my mouth down to the base.

I knew he was enjoying the sweet sensation as long as he could, but his dick was soon exploding down my throat. I swallowed every drop, which always pleased him and then continued sucking him until he was completely dry.

We hadn't been conscious of our surroundings for a long time, so we were nervously looking around to see if we had drawn an audience luckily, we hadn't. We caught our breaths as we stood and held each other close. It was getting dark and I really thought it was best that we got going, so we quickly put on our clothes, picked up our belongings and climbed back to where we parked. We really had no idea if the looks we received were in appreciation or envy.

Looking into each other's eyes, we knew we had just enjoyed something that would stay with us for the rest of our lives. We kissed deeply and proceeded to our car. Once we got home I found out I had forgotten my panties and it left a wicked smile on my face, because all I could think about was that somebody would have a souvenir from the new head bitch in charge, Ms. E'mani Newman.

Keith Williams

Chapter 24

Sweatt

Things had been starting to get real crazy for me since Mr. Montoya had been killed. I mean, the streets were hungry, and I was running dry on work so I did what any hustler would do in my situation. I started buying from Mr. Montoya's eldest son, Alex. The good part about doing business with Alex is that his prices were much cheaper than Mr. Montoya's and honestly, I really think the grade of the dope is better too but I felt like I was sighing my soul over to the devil by fucking with him.

My main man, Won Won, sat behind the wheel of our rented, smoke gray 2019 Buick Regal, while I rode shotgun on our way to Orlando to see Alex. The ride went smooth as a brick of cocaine, once we jumped on Interstate 75and drove straight there, only stopping to gas up and get back on the road. It took us two hours to get there and then another thirty minutes to get to Pine Hills.

Our connect, Alex, a chubby Cuban with curly hair who reminded me a little of the dude who owned the rim shop on the movie, *Blue Streak*, pulled up in a black Yukon. He had three big Haitians, the size of The Rock in the movie *Rundown*, right behind him. Even though he had been dealing with us long enough, I knew he still had a hard time trusting people, young black people even more, so he always told us to meet him where he would have the advantage.

Once everybody made it inside the apartment, where there was only a dining room table and triple beam digital scale, we got right down to business.

"How has business been treating the two of you?" Alex asked, while smoking on a Cuban cigar with his right leg across his left. We both knew Alex knew what was going on from our end, because unlike his father, he kept tabs on all his customers, but he loved hearing it from the horse's mouth.

"Business been going really good. I mean, how can it not? The dope is the best I've ever had my hands on, and the prices are what I've been asking God for all my life," I replied, sitting across from him. Alex sat quietly. I was hoping he wasn't thinking about raising the prices after seeing all the money I was making him, because I'd hate to have to go through it with him.

"Well, just to let you all know, I already know how much you're pulling in on a weekly basis and I'm pleased to hear you have my money. That's a good look for you, but I'm going to give a little word of advice," Alex stopped looking at his men before continuing. "When you're flamboyant, wearing all that shining jewelry every second of the day, you become the target of every stick-up kid on the prowl and I'd hate to have you come to me one day without my money. Now, that would be a bad look for you." With that said, Alex sat back in his chair. I thought hard about what he said but kept a straight face, while continuing business.

"I can have some of my people go to Gainesville and shoot first and ask questions later, while watching your back if you want?" Alex asked, more so making a suggestion. We both declined, more out of the embarrassment it would cause then anything. We didn't need Alex to think we couldn't handle our own problems, because we could and would, soon as they came our way.

A couple minutes passed before we gave Alex the duffle bag containing the money we owed, plus what we planned to cop with. Like always, we set up a time for the next day to pick up the work, before heading for the door. Alex suggested again about our situation, meaning sending his men to our city ad again we both declined his offering, saying we could handle ourselves.

In the car, we both thought about what Alex said again and personally, I really felt like he was disrespecting us. I knew how some Cubans could be racist as hell and only dealt with niggas because it benefited them, but that Chico that was really close to me ending his career, and that's on God! Won Won jumped in the passenger seat and reclined all the way back as I drove us to the Hilton and that let me know he was tired from driving all the way here.

We both asked for upstairs rooms, which we got after tipping the lady at the front desk, because our good looks wasn't making it happen. And to make it even better, they turned out to be right next to each other. I slept for a couple hours before I was awakened by my ringing cell phone. Not wanting to be bothered, I let it ring three or four more times before I answered.

"Who dis?"

"Nigga, get yo tired ass up, you know who the fuck this is. It's the Grim Reaper," Won Won said soon as I answered.

"What the fuck the Grim Reaper doing calling my phone, unless he got my money? I don't discriminate, I'll kill the walking dead too and that's on God," I shot back, now wide awake. I got out of bed and got myself together while Won Won talked shit on the other end of the phone. I started to hang up, but before I could, I heard the dial tone in my ear and laughed to myself. I grabbed my gun, tucking it in my waist grabbed some money then went next door to give his ass the whole clip for hanging up on me. We both had key cards to each other's rooms, so I didn't have to wait for him to let me in as I caught his ass slipping, watching girls twerking in music videos, while at the same time counting money. I dived on his ass before putting him in the head lock. He knew he had been caught and I could feel his body going with the motion as I leaned all the way back.

"Tap out, jit, before I put yo ass to sleep, we both know you ain't stronger than me," I said, while applying a little more pressure to my chokehold. He grabbed my arms, trying to minimize the pressure but the more he resisted, the more pressure I applied. Coughing and barely able to breathe, he tapped my arm repeatedly.

"I tapped, nigga! I tapped, let me the fuck go!" he shouted. I let go and just smiled while he caught his breath. "Man, you weak as fuck and had to sneak me. If I was ready, you wouldn't have tried that shit, because you know I'll bust yo ass," Won Won said.

"Nigga, I saw your eyes, you was about to cry like a little bitch. I bet you'll think twice about talking all that big boy shit next time and then hanging up on me," I replied, grabbing a Coke out of the mini fridge before flopping down on the bed. We talked for another fifteen minutes trying to figure out what our plans for the day because staying cooped up in this room wasn't gone happen.

"Damn bruh, shit starting to look real good for us. It seems as if Alex's really taking a liking to us, that muthafucka know we gone move that work and make him more of a millionaire than he probably is. But, on some real shit, if it wasn't for his daddy fucking with us before he died, Alex wouldn't have shit to do with us and probably would've had us killed for being in his way," Won Won said, staring off into space like he always does. "So, the best thing we could do in this situation is, make all the money we can and get the fuck out of his way, because something telling me he can't be trusted."

I just sat there and listened because I knew how he felt inside. I felt the same way, but since this was our only connect at the time, we had to put all our issues behind us and get this money, I still needed to try and get my sister off all them damn charges she was facing.

We walked out the door headed to the car and out the blue, a white Nissan Maxima crept up behind us. Out of habit, I reached for my gun not knowing the car. But I just as quickly relaxed when I saw the two females inside, once the driver rolled down the window.

"Excuse me, do y'all know where we can find the Hilton Hotel?" the driver asked. I looked around to see if I was going crazy and excuse my French, but I know these bitches saw that big ass sign that said the Hilton Hotel when they drove up.

"This is it right here, so look no further," I responded, pointing to the sign behind us and biting my tongue on what I really wanted to say.

"Girl, I told you this was it, but no… you ain't want to listen to me," the passenger said to the driver. While they argued back and forth about who was right, Won Won and I started walking off.

"Hold up a minute, we need help with something else," the driver shouted, stopping us in our tracks. "Do you know where we can find rooms 222 and 223?" Won Won and I both looked at each other in a suspicious manner, while at the same time, wondering who the hell these bitches were and what they were doing looking for our rooms.

"Who y'all looking for in those rooms?" I asked, knowing damn well we never met these girls before, so why would they be looking for us? The driver slightly shot me a unit before acting like the typical hood bitch that had no home training.

"We're not looking for you, so why you're concerned?"

I smiled to lighten up the situation, because I noticed she was getting a little defensive by the way she started rolling her neck, like she was trying to look at her ear without a mirror. "My bad, baby, I didn't mean it like that. I was just wondering, because those are our rooms y'all looking for," I responded.

"Are you fuckin serious right now? I mean, could your day get any worse? All I want to do is get some damn sleep," the driver complained while laughing to herself like she was crazy. It really was a coincidence that these girls ended up with the same rooms as us, but if anybody asked me, I saw it as a blessing from God because these bitches were double-dose twins fine.

"Well, I have a suggestion but before I put it out there, how about we introduce ourselves so we would at least know each other's names," I said, before continuing. "My name is Sweatt and this my homie, Won Won. We're just here on business and will most likely be gone in the morning." The driver smiled wickedly like she had just received the opportunity to make one of her sexual fantasies come true, before introducing herself as Aniyah and then pointing to the passenger and introducing her as her sister Ashley.

"We just moved here from Brooklyn, New York, and they're not completely done with our house yet, so they put us in this hotel for two days." Once we knew a little about each other, I suggested the girls stay with us for the two days to get to know each other better. Aniyah smiled her wicked smile again, before eyeing her sister to see what she thought about everything and to our surprise, Ashley shrugged her shoulders indicating she didn't have a problem with it.

With our arrangements now settled, they parked their car as Won Won and I played the gentlemanly role by carrying their bags to the rooms. Aniyah crashed with me while Ashley laid up with Won Won. We left that choice up to them to figure out, but I would've been happy either way. With everything that was going on, Aniyah was now nowhere near sleepy so we all bunched up in my room and smoked blunt after blunt of Loud until they couldn't handle any more. We were so fucking high, all we did was stare at each other for a whole ten minutes, until I heard Won Won trying to shoot his shot.

"Ashley, I know you and your sister about that, so I'm not gone beat around the bush. What's up with that esophagus?" We all laughed due to the effect of the weed but Won Won and I were probably the only two who really knew what he was talking about.

"Boy, what you mean?" Ashley asked, finally calming down from laughing so hard.

"Never mind, you probably wouldn't know what to do anyway," Won Won shot back, playing it off while still laughing. Won Won and I both knew if he would've told them what it meant, they probably would've gone from zero to a hundred real quick, no questions asked. It was about 2:30 in the morning when Won Won and Ashley went to their room and I can't lie, I was happy as hell they got the fuck out, because the effect of weed had Aniyah's hormones racing out of control.

She told me she was so horny that every time she took a step, the fabric of her panties would brush up against her clit sending electric shocks up her spine, causing her to have an orgasm. My dick instantly stood at attention and I gave her my skillful tongue treatment, aka this golden head, before dicking her down into a deep coma-like sleep.

Hours later, Won Won and I both got our things together and told the girls what the deal was, before getting their numbers and promising to keep in touch. We met back up with Alex, in the same spot as we had the day before and got straight own to business. The three big Haitians were told to pack all four duffle bags containing the work into the trunk of the Buick, under the spare tire. Once everything was taken care of and everybody was happy, Alex sent us on our way. Well, more like dismissed us like some bitches.

Chapter 25

Kendra

There was a lot of speculation going around that Sweatt was the reason Mahogany was facing the death penalty. I mean, I really didn't think he would do that to his only sister, but E'mani sure did and she sent me to Gainesville to investigate. Without further instructions, I knew just what to do and how I would do it. In every circle, there's a square hanging around who had the potential of having loose lips, you just had to find him.

So, it felt like the good old days all over again as I followed my prey and set my trap up. Once I saw his money green Impala SS stop at the light on Waldo Road and University Avenue, I crossed the street, walking right in front of his car in the tightest mini skirt I could find, making sure he saw the bottom of my ass as I swung my hips on my way inside McDonald's fast food restaurant.

"Welcome to McDonald's, how may I take your order?" the young girl at the cash register greeted me. Now, I was very confident in myself when it came to getting a man's attention, so it didn't surprise me at all when the second part of my plan fell in place, once the front door of McDonald's opened for the second time in five seconds.

"May I have a number three with no onions, large fries and a diet Coke please?" I ordered, trying to keep it simple. The cashier asked if I would like to try their new ranch and bacon McSandwich, but my shape was my attention grabber, so I denied her offer before she continued.

"Alright ma'am, your order will be five dollars and thirty cents." I pulled my skirt further down over my ass, knowing the man behind me was looking, before reaching into my purse for the cash to pay for my food.

"I got you, baby girl, if you don't mind?" I heard him say before I peeped over my shoulders, looking right into his eyes.

"No, I don't mind, you can pay for it. Besides, what woman in her right mind will turn down something free?" I responded. He gave the cashier a ten-dollar-bill before turning to me and introducing himself.

"My name is Ja'won, but everybody calls me Won Won," he said with his hand out for me to shake it. I stared him down as if he was HIV positive and I would catch it, before coming back to reality.

"I'm sorry, how rude of me, my name is Kendra and it's very nice to meet you." I shook his hand and we talked for a couple minutes, then I grabbed my food, thanked him and walked out the door. Like all men in their right mind, he knew a bad bitch when he saw one and wasn't going to let me get away that easy. So soon as I stepped out the door, he was right on my ass.

"What would you say if I told you I wanted to get to know you?" he asked.

I smiled, showing every last pearly white tooth in my mouth as I responded. "I would ask you in what way would you like to get to know me and—"

"In every way a man can get to know a woman. Mentally, physically, emotionally and even spiritually," he shot back, while cutting me off in the middle of my sentence. I glowed like the sun on a hot day because honestly, he surprised the hell out of me with his answer. I really wasn't expecting that.

"That's a really good answer and if you're really interested in getting to know me, like you said, how about giving me a ride home?" I then hopped in his car, not waiting on his answer before he did the same and drove off.

"I don't know why I let Sweatt talk me into helping him set Mahogany up with that Mr. Montoya bullshit," Won Won confessed to me after feeling the effects of the gram of Molly I slipped in his drink. Once we'd gotten to my house, I invited him in for a drink and like any trap, once you get caught in it, you're good as gone.

"I heard about that case, but everybody knows Rue set Mahogany up, that's why he was killed and—"

"That's what Sweatt wanted everybody to think. Sweatt's my main man so I would know, but if anybody would've sat down and actually dissected the whole ordeal, they'd know the truth. Yeah, Rue went after Mr. Montoya, but how do you think he knew exactly where Mr. Montoya lived or how to get in to kill his people? Think about it, Sweatt is the reason Mahogany is facing the death penalty right now," Won Won explained, cutting me off for the second time.

I was shocked to say the least, but I smiled, thinking about everything he had just told me, and now that I had everything I needed, it was time to take things to the next level. "Won Won, would you like some more Grey Goose?" I offered, walking towards the kitchen.

"Yeah but hold the ice and just fill it up halfway," he responded. I did as I was told before taking a shot myself, then taking him his glass.

"Here you go," I said, handing it to him. "I'm about to go slip into something a little more comfortable, if you don't mind, so don't get too drunk before I come back." Won Won looked at me and smiled, watching my ass as I walked off. Soon as I entered my room, I locked the door behind me and grabbed my cell phone to make a much-needed call. The phone rang twice, before a female with a soft tone answered.

"E'mani speaking!"

"Cousin, what's up? This Kendra," I said.

"Hey girl, it's about time you called a bitch. You had me a little worried," E'mani squealed excitedly. I took a deep breath to prepare myself, because I knew she would love to hear what I had to say. While at the same time, she wouldn't like what I had to say.

"I got ya boy Won Won in my apartment right now, and guess what? He did have something to do with Mahogany getting jammed. Him and Sweatt set the whole thing up with Rue." Once I finished, I waited to hear what her reaction would be, but I knew she knew Sweatt was guilty, because she said it in the beginning, I just didn't believe her.

"Thanks, Kendra. I knew I could count on you, but how you get him to talk? You must have given that nigga some pussy," E'mani stated.

"Not yet, but I plan on giving his sexy ass some before he die," I laughed, "but I just gave his ass a glass of Grey Goose after slipping a gram of Molly in that bitch and the next thing I know, he was talking like he just found out he had a voice." I walked to the door, unlocked it before peeping out. Seeing that Won Won was relaxing on the couch and rolling a blunt, I smiled to myself for being so nervous.

"Cousin, I also called to ask if I could handle this for you?" I asked and prayed she would say yes.

"No, Kendra! You know how I feel about you and Keira getting to deep in this shit and being that y'all just graduated, no! Not gone happen," she replied, and I could tell by the tone of her voice she was serious.

"But cousin, I can handle myself. Let me show you because right now I got this nigga eating out the palm of my hand," I pleaded. I knew E'mani loved me to death and would be devastated if something happened to me, but I'm not a teenager anymore. Even though Dontay told her to keep me far away from this lifestyle as much as she could, I would always find my way back to it, wanting to prove to her that she picked to right bitch to join her as a Baller Baby.

"Alright, you can handle it this time, only because I know you learned from the best. But," she stopped, took a deep breath then continued. "Kendra! Be careful."

"Oh, my God! Thank you, cousin," I shouted excitedly. "I promise, I'll be careful, and I won't let you down." I hung up, ready to get started and show E'mani that I could handle shit like a boss bitch.

Once I threw the phone on the bed, I began to undress. I then slowly rubbed my naked body down with my cotton-candy-scented lotion by Christian Dior. I didn't want to waste too much time. My plan was simple, fuck his brains out, catch my nut and then send him to an early grave, so I passed on wearing panties and just slid on my see-through teddy. When I felt it was showtime, I unlocked the door and called him.

"Won Won, would you come in here for a second?" I yelled. He stumbled into the room and I could clearly see he was feeling the effect of the liquor, the marijuana and the gram of Molly. I smiled at his expression, then took hold of his hand and led him to the bed, before placing mine on his chest and pushing him onto his back.

"Now, lay back, relax and enjoy yourself," I said as I untied my teddy and let it drop to the floor. He immediately released his erect dick from its prison while his eyes stayed on me. I then slowly crawled onto the bed in between his legs and slid my tongue up the length of his dick and down my throat once I reached the head.

"Mmmm…" he moaned softly as his eyes slowly closed. He then grabbed the back of my head as he guided himself in and out of my mouth. "Suck me, baby, damn it feels good," he whispered. I sucked until I felt that he was ready to come, then I stopped. "What's up, baby, why you stop?" he asked, after opening his eyes, clearly disappointed.

"I wasn't ready for you to come yet," I said, staring up at him and guided his dick into my wet and throbbing pussy.

"Oh God, it's big!" I cried out in pain, but it was quickly replaced with pleasure as I got into my rhythm and rode him for what his dick was worth.

"That's it, baby… get this pussy! Shit… Mmmm! I feel you, baby, I feel it," I moaned. He held onto my small waist as I bounced up and down on him, speeding up as my pussy got wetter. I could tell he loved how tight my walls were and me being so wet was a bonus.

"Damn, you got some good pussy!" he shouted.

"You like it, baby?" I asked, already knowing the answer.

"Mmm… shit, yeah!"

"Well, fuck me like it's the best you ever had." Now, it felt like I was going fifty mph as I was coming down on his dick with so much force and that's all it took. "Oh, shit, I'm about to cum! Baby, it's coming, fuck me harder." I came so hard and so much, it felt like a wave pool as my walls closed around his dick. Now that I had gotten my rocks off, Won Won pumped even faster to get his and the way my pussy was gripping, it wouldn't be long.

"Stop! That's enough, my stomach. I can't take it anymore," I moaned as I lifted myself off of him, then proceeded to put back on my teddy.

"What the fuck, Kendra!" he shouted as his nostrils flared revealing he was disappointed.

"I'm sorry, baby, but you're just too big. I couldn't take it anymore," I said, before walking out the room. *Bitch ass nigga, you're about to meet your maker anyway, so it doesn't matter that you didn't get yours*, I thought, as I entered the kitchen. I searched the drawers for my peacemaker and once I found it, I seductively walked back to the room and shot him four times in the head, while he masturbated on my bed sheets.

Nasty muthafucka, I thought as I called E'mani back to order a clean-up crew, because shit just got real. I stared at Won Won's motionless body as I gritted my teeth, because I knew I had just started a war with Sweatt and their crew. But I didn't give two fucks, because I was confident the Baller Babies would make bitches remember how much weight our name carried, period! Catch us outside, bitch.

To Be Continued...
Loyalty Ain't Promised 3
Coming Soon

Submission Guideline

Submit the first three chapters of your completed manuscript to ldpsubmissions@gmail.com, subject line: Your book's title. The manuscript must be in a .doc file and sent as an attachment. Document should be in Times New Roman, double spaced and in size 12 font. Also, provide your synopsis and full contact information. If sending multiple submissions, they must each be in a separate email.

Have a story but no way to send it electronically? You can still submit to LDP/Ca$h Presents. Send in the first three chapters, written or typed, of your completed manuscript to:

LDP: Submissions Dept
Po Box 944
Stockbridge, Ga 30281

DO NOT send original manuscript. Must be a duplicate.

Provide your synopsis and a cover letter containing your full contact information.

Thanks for considering LDP and Ca$h Presents.

KING OF THE TRAP II

By **T.J. Edwards**

GORILLAZ IN THE BAY V

De'Kari

THE STREETS ARE CALLING II

Duquie Wilson

KINGPIN KILLAZ IV

STREET KINGS III

PAID IN BLOOD III

CARTEL KILLAZ IV

DOPE GODS III

Hood Rich

SINS OF A HUSTLA II

ASAD

KINGZ OF THE GAME VI

Playa Ray

SLAUGHTER GANG IV

RUTHLESS HEART IV

By Willie Slaughter

THE HEART OF A SAVAGE III

By Jibril Williams

FUK SHYT II

By Blakk Diamond

THE REALEST KILLAZ III

By Tranay Adams

TRAP GOD III

By Troublesome

YAYO IV

GHOST MOB

Stilloan Robinson

Keith Williams

KINGPIN DREAMS III
By Paper Boi Rari
CREAM II
By Yolanda Moore
SON OF A DOPE FIEND III
By Renta
FOREVER GANGSTA II
GLOCKS ON SATIN SHEETS III
By Adrian Dulan
LOYALTY AIN'T PROMISED III
By Keith Williams
THE PRICE YOU PAY FOR LOVE II
By Destiny Skai
CONFESSIONS OF A GANGSTA II
By Nicholas Lock
I'M NOTHING WITHOUT HIS LOVE II
SINS OF A THUG II
By Monet Dragun
LIFE OF A SAVAGE IV
A GANGSTA'S QUR'AN III
MURDA SEASON III
GANGLAND CARTEL II
By **Romell Tukes**
QUIET MONEY III
THUG LIFE II
By **Trai'Quan**
THE STREETS MADE ME III
By **Larry D. Wright**
THE ULTIMATE SACRIFICE VI
IF YOU CROSS ME ONCE II

ANGEL III

By **Anthony Fields**

FRIEND OR FOE III

By **Mimi**

SAVAGE STORMS II

By **Meesha**

BLOOD ON THE MONEY II

By J-Blunt

THE STREETS WILL NEVER CLOSE II

By K'ajji

NIGHTMARES OF A HUSTLA II

By King Dream

Available Now

RESTRAINING ORDER **I & II**

By **CA$H & Coffee**

LOVE KNOWS NO BOUNDARIES **I II & III**

By **Coffee**

RAISED AS A GOON I, II, III & IV

BRED BY THE SLUMS I, II, III

BLAST FOR ME I & II

ROTTEN TO THE CORE I II III

A BRONX TALE I, II, III

DUFFEL BAG CARTEL I II III IV

Keith Williams

HEARTLESS GOON I II III IV

A SAVAGE DOPEBOY I II

HEARTLESS GOON I II III

DRUG LORDS I II III

CUTTHROAT MAFIA I II

By **Ghost**

LAY IT DOWN **I & II**

LAST OF A DYING BREED

BLOOD STAINS OF A SHOTTA I & II III

By **Jamaica**

LOYAL TO THE GAME I II III

LIFE OF SIN I, II III

By **TJ & Jelissa**

BLOODY COMMAS I & II

SKI MASK CARTEL I II & III

KING OF NEW YORK I II,III IV V

RISE TO POWER I II III

COKE KINGS I II III IV

BORN HEARTLESS I II III IV

KING OF THE TRAP

By **T.J. Edwards**

IF LOVING HIM IS WRONG…I & II

LOVE ME EVEN WHEN IT HURTS I II III

By **Jelissa**

WHEN THE STREETS CLAP BACK I & II III

THE HEART OF A SAVAGE I II

By **Jibril Williams**

A DISTINGUISHED THUG STOLE MY HEART I II & III

LOVE SHOULDN'T HURT I II III IV

RENEGADE BOYS I II III IV

PAID IN KARMA I II III

SAVAGE STORMS

By **Meesha**

A GANGSTER'S CODE I &, II III

A GANGSTER'S SYN I II III

THE SAVAGE LIFE I II III

CHAINED TO THE STREETS I II III

BLOOD ON THE MONEY

By J-Blunt

PUSH IT TO THE LIMIT

By **Bre' Hayes**

BLOOD OF A BOSS **I, II, III, IV, V**

SHADOWS OF THE GAME

By **Askari**

THE STREETS BLEED MURDER **I, II & III**

THE HEART OF A GANGSTA I II& III

By **Jerry Jackson**

CUM FOR ME I II III IV V VI

An **LDP Erotica Collaboration**

BRIDE OF A HUSTLA **I II & II**

THE FETTI GIRLS **I, II& III**

CORRUPTED BY A GANGSTA I, II III, IV

BLINDED BY HIS LOVE

THE PRICE YOU PAY FOR LOVE

DOPE GIRL MAGIC I II III

By **Destiny Skai**

WHEN A GOOD GIRL GOES BAD

By **Adrienne**

THE COST OF LOYALTY I II III

By Kweli

Keith Williams

A GANGSTER'S REVENGE **I II III & IV**

THE BOSS MAN'S DAUGHTERS I II III IV V

A SAVAGE LOVE **I & II**

BAE BELONGS TO ME I II

A HUSTLER'S DECEIT I, II, III

WHAT BAD BITCHES DO I, II, III

SOUL OF A MONSTER I II III

KILL ZONE

A DOPE BOY'S QUEEN I II

By **Aryanna**

A KINGPIN'S AMBITON

A KINGPIN'S AMBITION **II**

I MURDER FOR THE DOUGH

By **Ambitious**

TRUE SAVAGE I II III IV V VI

DOPE BOY MAGIC I, II, III

MIDNIGHT CARTEL I II

CITY OF KINGZ

By **Chris Green**

A DOPEBOY'S PRAYER

By **Eddie "Wolf" Lee**

THE KING CARTEL **I, II & III**

By **Frank Gresham**

THESE NIGGAS AIN'T LOYAL **I, II & III**

By **Nikki Tee**

GANGSTA SHYT **I II &III**

By **CATO**

THE ULTIMATE BETRAYAL

By **Phoenix**

BOSS'N UP **I , II & III**

Loyalty Ain't Promised 2

By **Royal Nicole**

I LOVE YOU TO DEATH

By Destiny J

I RIDE FOR MY HITTA

I STILL RIDE FOR MY HITTA

By **Misty Holt**

LOVE & CHASIN' PAPER

By **Qay Crockett**

TO DIE IN VAIN

SINS OF A HUSTLA

By **ASAD**

BROOKLYN HUSTLAZ

By **Boogsy Morina**

BROOKLYN ON LOCK I & II

By **Sonovia**

GANGSTA CITY

By **Teddy Duke**

A DRUG KING AND HIS DIAMOND I & II III

A DOPEMAN'S RICHES

HER MAN, MINE'S TOO I, II

CASH MONEY HO'S

By Nicole Goosby

TRAPHOUSE KING **I II & III**

KINGPIN KILLAZ I II III

STREET KINGS I II

PAID IN BLOOD **I II**

CARTEL KILLAZ I II III

DOPE GODS I II

By **Hood Rich**

LIPSTICK KILLAH **I, II, III**

Keith Williams

CRIME OF PASSION I II & III

FRIEND OR FOE I II

By **Mimi**

STEADY MOBBN' **I, II, III**

THE STREETS STAINED MY SOUL

By **Marcellus Allen**

WHO SHOT YA **I, II, III**

SON OF A DOPE FIEND I II

Renta

GORILLAZ IN THE BAY **I II III IV**

TEARS OF A GANGSTA I II

DE'KARI

TRIGGADALE I II III

Elijah R. Freeman

GOD BLESS THE TRAPPERS I, II, III

THESE SCANDALOUS STREETS I, II, III

FEAR MY GANGSTA I, II, III IV, V

THESE STREETS DON'T LOVE NOBODY I, II

BURY ME A G I, II, III, IV, V

A GANGSTA'S EMPIRE I, II, III, IV

THE DOPEMAN'S BODYGAURD I II

THE REALEST KILLAZ I II

Tranay Adams

THE STREETS ARE CALLING

Duquie Wilson

MARRIED TO A BOSS... I II III

By Destiny Skai & Chris Green

KINGZ OF THE GAME I II III IV V

Playa Ray

SLAUGHTER GANG I II III

RUTHLESS HEART I II III

By Willie Slaughter

FUK SHYT

By Blakk Diamond

DON'T F#CK WITH MY HEART I II

By Linnea

ADDICTED TO THE DRAMA I II III

By Jamila

YAYO I II III

A SHOOTER'S AMBITION I II

By S. Allen

TRAP GOD I II

By Troublesome

FOREVER GANGSTA

GLOCKS ON SATIN SHEETS I II

By Adrian Dulan

TOE TAGZ I II III

By Ah'Million

KINGPIN DREAMS I II

By Paper Boi Rari

CONFESSIONS OF A GANGSTA

By Nicholas Lock

I'M NOTHING WITHOUT HIS LOVE

SINS OF A THUG

By Monet Dragun

CAUGHT UP IN THE LIFE I II III

By Robert Baptiste

NEW TO THE GAME I II III

By **Malik D. Rice**

LIFE OF A SAVAGE I II III

Keith Williams

A GANGSTA'S QUR'AN I II

MURDA SEASON I II

GANGLAND CARTEL

By **Romell Tukes**

LOYALTY AIN'T PROMISED I II

By Keith Williams

QUIET MONEY I II

THUG LIFE

By **Trai'Quan**

THE STREETS MADE ME I II

By **Larry D. Wright**

THE ULTIMATE SACRIFICE I, II, III, IV, V

KHADIFI

IF YOU CROSS ME ONCE

ANGEL I II

By **Anthony Fields**

THE LIFE OF A HOOD STAR

By Ca$h & Rashia Wilson

THE STREETS WILL NEVER CLOSE

By K'ajji

CREAM

By Yolanda Moore

NIGHTMARES OF A HUSTLA

By King Dream

BOOKS BY LDP'S CEO, CA$H

TRUST IN NO MAN

TRUST IN NO MAN 2

TRUST IN NO MAN 3

BONDED BY BLOOD

SHORTY GOT A THUG

THUGS CRY

THUGS CRY 2

THUGS CRY 3

TRUST NO BITCH

TRUST NO BITCH 2

TRUST NO BITCH 3

TIL MY CASKET DROPS

RESTRAINING ORDER

RESTRAINING ORDER 2

IN LOVE WITH A CONVICT

LIFE OF A HOOD STAR

Keith Williams